WARRIOR ANGEL

HER ANGEL: BOUND WARRIORS
BOOK 3

FELICITY HEATON

THE HER ANGEL WORLD

HER ANGEL: BOUND WARRIORS
Book 1: Dark Angel
Book 2: Fallen Angel
Book 3: Warrior Angel
Book 4: Bound Angel

HER ANGEL: ETERNAL WARRIORS
Book 1: Her Guardian Angel
Book 2: Her Demonic Angel
Book 3: Her Wicked Angel
Book 4: Her Avenging Angel
Book 5: Her Sinful Angel

Discover more available paranormal romance books at:
http://www.felicityheaton.com

Or sign up to my mailing list to receive a FREE vampire romance ebook,
learn about new titles, be eligible for special subscriber-only giveaways, and
read exclusive content including short stories:
http://ml.felicityheaton.com/mailinglist

CHAPTER 1

She was heading for trouble.

Einar watched the raven-haired woman walking straight towards a male coming the opposite way through the moonlit park. He beat his tawny wings, keeping his position high above them in the cool air.

The woman appeared and disappeared as she passed under the intermittent streetlamps that lined the paths that snaked through the London park like veins, arteries that had grown quiet over the past hour as night had tightened its hold on the city. The lights used in an attempt to offer guidance and safety through the enormous area of green weren't strong enough to cut through the darkness, leaving the park as a black hole in a sea of glittering golden and white pinpricks.

London stretched as far as he could see in all directions, a golden halo capping it that drowned out the stars and revealed the shadowy shapes of the high-rises and landmarks to him.

Einar swooped lower in the night, wanting to get a better look at the two people and unable to ignore the pressing need to be closer in case he was right and the man wasn't a man at all.

If the demon showed any sign of attacking the woman, he would intervene. Until that happened, he would watch, hidden from them both by his power.

It wasn't his place to interfere in things.

He was here to hunt, not protect.

The steady rush of wind over him chilled his skin, drawing his focus to the world around him again, even as he tried to keep it pinned on the female and the potential demon below him.

Summer was on its way out and autumn was encroaching as surely as the night. The days were growing short and he still hadn't found his demon targets, despite scouring the city for them, chasing every lead he had and every new one he discovered.

Heaven's Court were becoming restless with the desire to know why a commander of theirs called Amaer had sided with three demons, assisting them in the disposal of over one hundred human bodies, and had incriminated a fellow angel, setting him up to take the fall.

Lukas hadn't deserved to have such a thing happen to him. For as long as Einar had known him, the mediator had been one of the most upstanding and loyal angels in Heaven. If Einar had known about his plight earlier, if his old comrade had told him what had happened and how he had been blamed for a crime he hadn't committed, he would have tried to help him sooner.

He had failed to help him clear his name and prove his innocence, but he wouldn't fail to find out what Amaer had been doing and he wouldn't fail to track down the demons who had been involved.

Although, Lukas could have helped him by keeping Amaer alive so Einar could question him. He sighed at that and shook his head. He couldn't blame Lukas. The male had been given an order, and he had fulfilled it, and Heaven hadn't exactly taken a back seat in proceedings. They had been the ones to obliterate Amaer.

Destroying any leads and information Amaer could have given him in the process.

Now his only lead were the demons.

Einar sensed the woman moving closer and his focus snapped back to her.

She was close to the man now.

Einar's hand went to the hilt of the blade hanging from his waist. The vambrace protecting his forearm was cold against the strip of stomach exposed between his rich brown and gold breastplate and the pointed strips of armour that protected his hips.

It wouldn't be long before he had to wear winter armour, which meant this hunt was taking too long. It was wearing him down now. He couldn't remember the last time he had slept for more than a few hours before waking, driven by a restlessness that demanded he keep searching for the demons and answers.

It was beginning to affect his concentration.

A noise from below snagged his attention. He silently cursed himself as the woman reared back as the man lunged for her, her black hair dancing in the breeze as she attempted to evade him.

Einar beat his wings and shot towards her.

Slammed to a halt in mid-air barely a few metres above her, unable to believe his eyes as she drew a short silver blade from beneath the back of her black jacket and started to fight.

She was breathtaking.

He could only stare as she fought the male demon who still wore his human form.

Her movements were fluid, mesmerising, made only more graceful by her slender figure and the tight clothes that hugged her long legs, trim waist and lean torso. She swung her right leg around, connecting hard with the demon's head, and the male grunted and snarled as he struggled to shake off the blow. The moment her foot touched the floor, she brought it back again, catching the demon unawares and unguarded.

He toppled sideways, losing balance and fighting to remain upright.

She kicked off on a low grunt, barrelling towards the demon and putting him on the back foot, keeping him off balance with lunges and swipes of the short blade.

It gleamed brightly in the moonlight, flashes of white and silver lines marking its deadly path.

Einar beat his wings to keep steady, bewitched by the woman and her ability to fight, unable to bring himself to move despite the need to help her that steadily built inside him.

He couldn't stop himself from admiring her, didn't want to disturb her or make her aware of him, because he feared it would end the alluring dance she was performing with her opponent.

He had never thought a female could have such skill.

He had only ever met females that needed tending to and protecting.

This one was different. She handled a weapon with ease, and with skill almost matching his own, and she radiated confidence and strength that said she could take care of herself. It didn't stop him from wanting to intervene in her fight, but he was damned if he could convince himself to move.

The male demon snarled and shifted his shoulders. Black ragged scaly wings erupted from his back, tearing through his dark shirt, and his hands became talons.

Einar's eyes narrowed.

The history recorded in the pool in Hell had revealed the type of demon that had committed the sin of killing the innocent humans.

This man was one of their breed.

Einar's dark gaze leaped to the woman, because he was sure she would be horrified, shocked or possibly even already fleeing, and he refused to let the demon get the jump on her, was ready to swoop down and assist her, taking over the battle against the male.

She didn't even hesitate at the sight of the man's wings and claws. She continued her attack, evading every lunge and swipe he made at her, dealing blows of her own in return whenever she could get close enough and showing no sign of running.

If anything, she was putting more effort into the fight now that the demon had revealed himself.

Which meant she wasn't a stranger to this sort of creature.

The demon screeched and launched himself at her, still half in his human guise. She blocked each slash of his talons with her short sword but the demon was forcing her backwards now, putting her off balance this time. She rallied, kicking the demon in the shin and then aiming another one at his chest.

Time seemed to slow as the demon grinned, easily caught her ankle and twisted, hurling her along the pavement. She tumbled, arms and legs flailing, her weapon flying across the grass, and stopped a few metres away from the demon. She was still for a moment, a heartbeat that seemed like an eternity to Einar as he focused on her, needing to see if she was hurt or worse, unconscious and vulnerable, and then she growled a dark curse.

Her long dark hair covered her face as she struggled to get to her feet.

Cold fury curled through Einar's veins, tightening his muscles. He flexed his fingers around the hilt of his sword and gripped it so tightly his bones hurt. He had seen enough.

The demon ran at the woman.

Einar swept down between them, dropping the glamour that concealed him from their eyes at the same time as he drew his sword, and blocked the demon's attack.

The male snarled and hissed through his fangs as he leaped backwards, placing some distance between them.

Einar pulled down a deep breath, steadying himself as he waited, holding the demon's dark gaze as the male stared at him, his expression constantly shifting as he studied Einar.

Was he thinking of running?

He wouldn't get far.

If he was thinking of attacking him, he would meet the same fate.

If he was thinking about reaching the woman to hurt her?

Einar needed the male alive, but he would kill the wretch if he had to in order to protect her. He stretched his tawny wings out to shield her where she struggled behind him. The rich smell of her blood filled the air as she muttered black things under her breath. The demon would pay for hurting her, after he had extracted information from him.

The urge to glance over his shoulder to check on her was powerful, consuming, but he denied it, keeping his focus on the demon instead. He would tend to her once he had dealt with the demon.

The male twitched.

Einar readied himself.

"Get out of my damn way, you big oaf," the woman bit out just as the demon charged them.

Einar turned towards her. Was she speaking to him?

She crouched, tugged the right leg of her dark jeans up, revealing her black leather boot, and the next thing Einar knew, she had a knife in her hand and was running past him.

Resilient, resourceful, but foolish.

Unless she wanted to get herself killed.

She lunged at the demon on a battle cry that stirred Einar's blood in a way he really didn't want to examine.

The demon lashed out, slamming the back of his right hand into the side of her head, sending her skidding across the dewy grass. She landed in a heap and didn't move this time. Einar beat his tawny wings and shot towards the demon, his blade aimed directly at the male. The demon barely had a chance to look at him before Einar's sword was through his gut, ripping a bellow from him. Einar locked gazes with the demon, clenched his jaw and twisted the sword, tearing another pained cry from him.

"Tell me where the others are hiding," Einar growled and the flicker of fear in the demon's eyes told him everything he needed to know. He was right. This demon was one of them. "Tell me, and you will live. Do not tell me, and I will banish you to Hell to face your master instead."

The demon's eyes widened and he shook his head.

He opened his mouth.

Strange cold rushed from below Einar's feet.

Before he could move, a column of darkness swept up and around them, engulfing both him and the demon. Intense heat and a vivid golden glow lit the ground beneath them as the column rapidly expanded and he tightened his grip on the demon as he felt power pushing at him.

He couldn't lose the male, couldn't lose the information he could give him, the lead he so desperately needed and felt sure this demon was about to offer him.

His boots lifted off the floor. His grip slipped.

Einar bit out an oath as a blast of the dark power flung him backwards, sending him tumbling heels over head into the sky. He stretched his wings out, gritted his teeth as they caught the currents and twisted painfully, and grinned as he managed to beat them, stopping his ascent.

He turned and plummeted back towards the demon.

A bright flash blinded him and he instinctively shielded his eyes.

When the light dissipated, he lowered his hand and stared down at where the demon had been.

A charred circle on the ground was all that remained, together with the sickening stench of brimstone hanging in the cool night air.

A dark curse rolled off Einar's tongue as he landed gently, sheathed his sword, and walked to the burnt patch of path. He crouched beside it, reached out and hovered his hand over the warm ashes. A sigh lifted his shoulders, causing his breastplate to shift.

Had someone done this to stop the demon from talking?

It wasn't the Devil. He took no interest in such affairs and Einar's threat had been just that—a threat. The Devil wouldn't do anything if Einar could banish a demon to Hell to face the consequences. If anything, he would probably congratulate the demon for doing something to annoy Heaven and the angels.

A groan from the darkness snapped Einar out of his thoughts. The woman. He twisted towards her.

She pressed her hands into the grass, her arms shaking as she tried to push herself up. Her tangled fall of dark hair swayed as she struggled, concealing her face from him but not her voice. She was still muttering obscenities, had a tongue a demon would be proud of as she managed to get onto her feet. The smell of blood grew stronger.

She touched her arm, brought her hand out in front of her, and promptly collapsed.

CHAPTER 2

Einar rushed over to the woman, falling to his knees beside her where she lay on the grass. "Are you alright?"

He leaned over and swept the messy ribbons of black hair from her face, clearing it so he could get a better look at her. She was pale, the moonlight turning her skin milky. Dark patches of blood marred it near her jaw and across her chest above the low line of her black top. He scanned for the place she had touched and stilled when he spotted it.

There were three long gashes in the right arm of her leather biker jacket. The demon. He must have caught her with his claws.

Einar slid his arm under her back and carefully lifted it off the wet grass, supporting her. She moaned and writhed, and then stilled, sinking against him.

He stilled too.

Stared down at her pale beauty, captivated by it as much as he had been by her fighting, bewitched all over again by her.

Perhaps he had been mistaken.

Perhaps he was the one heading for trouble.

He touched the blood on her cheek and frowned.

What was trouble's name?

Was it as beautiful as her looks and the way she fought?

She moaned, her fine dark eyebrows knitting and putting a furrow in her brow as her lips twisted.

Einar canted his head.

Was so fascinated by her that he missed the cue, or maybe she didn't give him one.

She suddenly lurched at him and tackled him to the ground, pinning his wings awkwardly beneath him.

He grimaced, gripped her waist and tried to get her off him so he could at least get them free. She growled, shoved his hands off her and pressed her full weight down onto his stomach, groin and chest, her strength surprising and enough to keep him pinned.

"Who the hell are you?" Her dark eyes were wild, watching him without fear but with anger. She wet her luscious full lips and frowned, her eyes losing focus for a moment as she shook her head. Her left hand slid off his damp breastplate and he instinctively caught her to stop her from falling. She grabbed his hand and pushed it away, fixing him with a deadly glare. "Get off me. Bloody angels. Always interfering."

She wavered, dipping forwards, pushing more weight down on his chest, and clenched her jaw.

Her eyes slipped shut and then shot open again.

"It's the toxin," Einar murmured in a low voice, not wanting to enrage her. She didn't seem to like angels for some reason and was clearly gifted in some way since she could see him for what he was. He rested his hands beside his head on the damp grass, trying to show her that he didn't intend to hurt her, and smiled in what he hoped was a winsome way. "I can fix that for you."

She glanced down at her right shoulder, something flashed in her hand and he froze as she pressed the knife against his throat. It trembled, touching his Adam's apple, and she blinked several times, as though trying to clear her head. It wasn't going to work. She couldn't just shake this off.

How long did she have?

Demon toxins worked fast.

"I don't need your help." She pushed off him, caught her boot on his hip as she stepped over him and stumbled across the grass in the empty moonlit park, half-slurring half-muttering, "Where's my fucking sword?"

Einar stood, stretched his wings and flapped them to get his feathers back into place. He frowned down at his wet backside and legs, and then cocked his head to one side and watched her.

Regardless of what she said, she did need his help.

The most virulent demon toxin only took a few minutes to work its way into blood and only another hour on top of that to spread through the body and kill the host. It was difficult to get rid of and he was certain she knew that.

What did she plan to do?

Human drugs had little effect on such poison. It would take another demon to remove it.

Was she in league with them? He hadn't wanted to believe such a thing when he had first seen her, but he couldn't deny that it was a possibility.

She stooped to pick up her sword and collapsed into a heap, landing on her face with her backside in the air.

Einar was beside her in an instant. He collected her blade, jammed it into his sword belt, and then grabbed hold of her. She didn't protest as he lifted her into his arms but she did mumble something that sounded like more cursing. He cursed himself too.

What was he doing? What if she was in league with demons, fraternised with them rather than merely hunting them?

He pushed those questions out of his head and focused on her slight weight in his arms, her rapid breathing and the way she was beginning to shake as the poison tightened its grip on her.

He didn't care what she had done before tonight, he wasn't going to let her go and seek the aid of demons now that he was here.

He froze.

Was he protecting her?

Why?

His gaze traversed her delicate face.

He was definitely heading for trouble.

It was forbidden for him to have any sort of feeling for her.

He stared at her a moment longer, torn between leaving her to find her own way of clearing the poison from her blood and taking her with him to his place and removing it for her. The hunter in him said to leave her. She wasn't worth anything and would only cause him trouble.

The man in him said to save her.

Einar closed his eyes, cradled her to his chest, and took flight.

He couldn't leave her to fend for herself. It didn't matter that Heaven forbid him to intervene in such matters or to feel anything for her. His heart whispered to help her and he would do just that. He would rid her body of the poison and restore her strength.

If anyone asked him why he had done such a thing, he would lie and say that he had done it for information.

Not because he was drawn to her.

She woke during the flight to his hotel. He kept his gaze on the rooftops of London, charting his course and checking it for any sign of trouble. The sky was his tonight, shared only with the constant circling planes above him as they waited to land at one of the busy airports. They were too high to bother him. He couldn't fly at that altitude when carrying mortal cargo. The air was too cold and too thin for such a fragile creature.

He glanced down at her, meeting her dark eyes.

They shone with something between confusion and anger.

"How are you feeling?" Einar fixed his gaze ahead again, sensing that if he continued to stare at her, she was likely to start fighting him and that it would only end badly.

For her.

"I'd feel a lot better if you put me down." She pushed his chest so quickly that he almost lost his grip on her. A heartbeat later, she was clutching the edges of his deep brown breastplate and curled up against him, fear pounding in her veins so strongly that he could sense it as though it was his own. "Christ Almighty, we're flying."

He smiled.

It touched his lips before he could even think to contain it.

She had made him smile.

Not a forced one as he generally managed, but a real smile.

He tightened his grip on her knees and her ribs, and swooped lower with her, so she wouldn't be afraid. He levelled off just above the hotchpotch rooftops and narrowed his eyes on the spot in the distance where the hotel was located.

"Keep going, Romeo, all the way down." She hooked her fingers over his breastplate near his shoulders and tugged at it, as though she could control his descent by doing such a thing and force him to land.

"I do not think so." Einar glanced at her again. "You are particularly resilient to demon toxin but you are in no fit state to be left alone. I will tend to you once we are somewhere safe."

"There's nowhere safe in this city," she mumbled softly, her eyes leaping around over the rooftops below them.

She twisted out of his arms.

Einar went after her on a curse. She turned and twirled in the air like a cat finding its footing during a fall and landed soundly on her feet on the flat roof of the building. Stupid woman. She made it ten steps before collapsing.

"Shit." She got to her feet and tried to run again, this time reaching the edge of the roof and balancing there, staring down into the street below.

"Where do you intend to run to?" He landed behind her and caught her arm, afraid that she would fall if he didn't do something and willing to risk her wrath to keep her safe.

She turned to look at him with wide eyes that spoke of fear, her lips parted and teasing him with temptation.

Desire tugged at his gut, foreign and powerful, a need he had to fight hard to deny and suppress.

He pulled her back into his arms, lifted her again and cradled her close to his chest.

His eyes fell to her mouth, the fire he had just vanquished blazing through him again as he stared at her lips, urging him to give in.

He forced his gaze up to meet hers. "You are in no fit state to run."

"I felt better." She frowned, looked herself over, and then met his eyes again. "And then I felt terrible."

He smiled for a second time. "It is my presence that staves off the toxin. The moment you were away from my touch, the infection returned. I do not intend to harm you... whoever you are."

She swallowed, blinked, and then rallied and looped her arms around his neck as she smiled saucily. "You don't get my name that easily, Romeo."

Einar looked down at her arms, a hot achy shiver burning down his spine when she tangled her fingers in the short threads of his ponytail. Her fingertips grazed his neck, sending another wave of tingles trickling over his skin, and her breath washed his face as she leaned in close, pulling herself up and pressing her cheek to his.

Her lips grazed his ear and he was lost, empty inside, unable to focus on anything but the feel of her against him and the anticipation of hearing her speak.

"You've got to tell a girl your name first," she whispered into his ear. Was it the toxin making her act so strangely, or was she always like this with men, so forward and teasing? "It's considered polite."

He closed his eyes, swallowed to ease his dry throat, and resisted his desire to clutch her to him, to hold her where she was so he could feel her body against his a moment longer.

"Einar." He breathed his name on a sigh, unable to find his voice for some reason.

What was she doing to him?

Was she temptation sent by the Devil to test him?

"Mmm, that's a strong name for a strong boy." She ran her hands down his biceps and they trembled under her soft touch. He shook when she cupped his cheeks, sending warmth racing through every inch of him, and drew back to look into his eyes. She smiled. "Now... put me the hell down!"

Her forehead cracked hard against his and he stumbled backwards, losing his grip on her.

Before he could grab her, she leaped to the next building and was running again.

Einar touched his forehead and frowned as his skull ached. Why was she running from him? Was she afraid that he was going to harm her? He had no intention of hurting her. He only wanted to help.

He stretched his wings and flew after her, keeping his distance this time. She would falter soon enough. He hadn't lied to her. It was only his touch and presence that slowed the effects of the poison on her body. He gave her a minute before she collapsed again and became compliant once more.

She didn't even last that long. Before she was halfway across the rooftop, she tripped and fell flat on her face. She didn't get back up. She lay there on the damp black tar roof, breathing hard.

Einar landed close beside her and she grabbed his ankle and looked up at him out of the corner of her eye, ribbons of her long hair cutting across her cheek.

She said something he couldn't make out. He crouched close to her and her hand skimmed up the gold-edged brown greave that protected his shin and settled on his bare knee.

"Maybe I'll take you up on that offer." Her words were so quiet that he barely heard her. She closed her eyes and sighed. "Not feeling myself today."

Einar was sure that when she was feeling herself, she was a force to be reckoned with. She had proven that much to him.

He carefully lifted her back into his arms, not surprised when she didn't fight him. She was limp in his embrace, lax against him, breathing softly and slowly. When he focused hard on her, he sensed her fatigue and how close she was to the edge now. She had only made things worse by trying to escape. Exerting herself had quickened the process of spreading the poison through her body.

She shivered and moaned.

"Taylor."

He frowned.

Her eyes fluttered open, their dark depths capturing his attention and holding it. She almost smiled. Her lips wobbled weakly.

"My name... it's Taylor." She closed her eyes and leaned her cheek against his shoulder and biceps.

Einar held her close to him and looked at her. Taylor.

A strong but beautiful name for a strong beautiful woman.

He took flight with her again, heading for the hotel and pondering this strange twist of fate that had brought her into his life. She was turning his world, distorting its axis, and he was sure of only one thing.

He was heading for trouble.

CHAPTER 3

Taylor shivered against Einar's broad breastplate as he carried her into the brightly lit cream foyer of a grand hotel. She peered through the dark curtain of her hair, keeping her face obscured to hide the blood on it. There were several humans in the room, and only the clerk glanced at them from behind his large polished wood and gold desk as Einar moved between the elegant cream marble columns, his boots loud on the pale floor as he headed towards the man.

The three who were sitting in one of the groups of plush dark red armchairs to her left, beyond the columns, paid them no heed.

She waited as they drew level with the group, sure someone would look her way.

They didn't even glance at her and Einar, which meant two things.

This was the sort of upmarket hotel where staff didn't ask questions, not even when a guest walked in at gone midnight carrying a woman as though she was a damsel in distress, and they couldn't see his wings.

He had paused outside and she knew he had been changing his appearance. When he had looked at her, she had feigned surprise, afraid that he would realise that she could see through his glamour and could still see his armour and his tawny wings.

Nothing good would happen if he knew his glamour didn't work on her.

She needed to get the poison out of her system, and this angel wasn't lying when he said that he could do such a thing for her. It was quicker and easier to let him tend to her than trying to find the local demon medic to get rid of it for her. She wasn't sure she had the luxury of time anymore.

She had been foolish.

Trying to run from him had quickened the spread of the poison through her body and it was on the verge of entering the final phase and killing her.

But fear had propelled her, pushed her to flee from him before he realised what she was and condemned her for it.

It still pushed her to flee.

Einar looked impatient as he stood in the wood-panelled elevator, heading upwards. His dark eyes remained locked on the numbers on the gold panel as they changed and she found the courage to study his face, the urge to flee fading now that his focus was away from her.

Did he know how deep the poison was in her body now? Would it be too late to save her?

Would it be?

Panic sparked to life inside her, gripped her in icy talons that felt as if they were squeezing the life out of her.

She couldn't stop herself from seizing hold of his chest armour, couldn't stop herself from gripping it as tightly as those talons of fear gripped her. Her breath rattled in her lungs, heart pounding as her head filled with images of her end, of the horrific way she was going to die. She had seen what demon toxins could do to people, had witnessed their terrible demise, and she didn't want to go through that.

She didn't want to die.

Einar slowly lowered his head, his eyes calmly locking with hers, and the moment they met, a strange sense of relief washed through her, loosened the grip fear had on her and chased away the terrifying visions of death. She focused on him, seized his gaze as fiercely as she had his breastplate, desperate to drive out the fear again.

"Just a few moments longer," he whispered, the soft deep sound of his voice soothing her. "Hold on."

His rich brown eyes held hers, as if he knew she needed him to keep looking at her, needed the distraction from what was happening. The flecks of gold in his eyes shifted in that way an angel's irises always did, but for once, it didn't frighten her.

It mesmerised her.

When she had met her first angel, their eyes had scared her more than the wings. Nothing about them felt real. It never had. They weren't of this world. They were something else.

Taylor looked deep into Einar's eyes.

He seemed real though, and looked handsome with his eyes brimming with concern and his grip on her tight and reassuring. He smiled when the lift pinged and the doors opened.

"Keep holding on," he said and she nodded, lost in his gaze.

He walked down a warmly-lit cream corridor with her, taking turns she didn't notice as she held on to him. When he stopped, she gripped him harder, as firmly as she could with her hands shaking so violently as he fumbled with the door, struggling to open it while holding her.

Her hands ached, muscles threatening to turn to water, so she moved them up and wrapped her arms around his neck.

Her fingers brushed his nape, grazing the strands of his short mousy ponytail, and she cursed herself for the way it affected her, had heat pouring through her as she recalled how she had teased him earlier. It was his fault. He had surprised her when she had pulled back and had seen in his eyes that it had affected him, had stirred desire in him.

She knew angels weren't saints, and that they were as frivolous and passionate as the next man when given the chance, but she hadn't expected him to be affected by her attention and touch.

Unable to resist seeing if it had just been a momentary slip on his part, Taylor pushed her fingers into his hair, loosening it from the band that kept it tied back at the nape of his neck.

The waves of golden brown fell down to caress his jaw and he stilled.

His gaze burned into her and she shyly met it, afraid of what she would see.

His eyes were brighter, golden like a raptor's, and fixed intently on her. His pupils widened when she curled his hair around her fingers and his lips parted. Desire filled his eyes again. She was affecting him.

Why?

It wasn't possible that he didn't know the secret she held in her heart and in her blood. It just wasn't possible.

But if he did, he wouldn't look at her with such fire and hunger.

He wouldn't look at her at all.

The door swung open.

Taylor got the better of herself and removed her hands from his neck, settling them in her lap as he adjusted his grip on her again. She stared at her knees, waiting for him to carry her inside.

He didn't move. He remained on the threshold of the hotel room, staring at her, his breathing heavy enough that she shifted with it in his arms.

What was he thinking as he looked at her? Did he burn with the same fierce and impossible needs as her? She shouldn't have teased him again, but she had wanted to see if that moment on the rooftop had been real. She wasn't sure why.

Pain speared her chest.

She flinched and pressed her hand to it.

It spurred Einar into moving and before she could blink, she was in a bedroom with him. She clutched her chest, burning inside for a different reason now, and breathed deep and steadily. She wasn't afraid. The angel would help her. Her hands trembled and her limbs shook. She wasn't afraid.

She wasn't.

Einar settled her on the white double bed and she curled up into a ball on her left side, gripping her right arm. She squeezed her eyes shut and clenched her jaw as pain ripped through her, blazing like an inferno, stealing her strength and leaving her shaking. She wasn't afraid.

Panic twisted her stomach.

Okay. She was afraid.

"Shh," Einar murmured softly and took hold of her hand.

She stared at it a moment, shock dancing through her at the feel of his strong hand encompassing hers, and then rolled onto her back, covered it with her other one and clung to him.

He was her only hope now.

The poison was too deep in her body.

If he couldn't save her, she wouldn't have time to find someone who could.

Einar moved her and she was too weak to fight him, wasn't sure she wanted to anymore. She wanted to surrender to him, to give up the fight and trust that he would take care of her. He stretched her out on the bed so she lay with her head on the soft downy pillows and her body in a straight line.

He ran a glance over her and met her gaze again. "Try to keep still."

Taylor's eyes widened when he held his hands out several inches above her, palms facing her, and, like a magician performing a trick, moved them back and forth along the length of her body.

And just like magic, a white light appeared, beaming down from his hands, blinding her.

She couldn't take her eyes off it though. They tracked it, unable to believe what she was seeing and feeling. Wherever the light touched, she felt warm, weightless, and better.

He moved his hands down to her feet and then back up her legs, over her arms and stomach, and then finally settled with one over her chest and one over her head.

"Look at me."

She obeyed the command in his deep voice and stared up into his eyes. They were golden now, bright and sharp, holding hers in a way that was impossible to break free from.

"Keep looking at me."

Taylor nodded.

A bright burst of light dulled her vision.

Excruciating pain stabbed her heart and head.

She gritted her teeth and arched off the bed, clutching the covers and bunching them into her fists.

Bloody hell.

It didn't hurt like this when demons took the poison out.

But then, she had never been this close to dying before.

She tried to remain conscious and keep her eyes on Einar, just as he had said, but dark waves crashed over her, pulling her under. The more she fought them, the stronger they grew, tugging at her, pressing down on her. She blinked and forced her eyes back open, looking at Einar where he stood over her, his focus on his hands and whatever hellish thing he was doing to her.

She couldn't hold on.

The waves battered her and she slipped, let them sweep her away because they would steal the pain away too.

She sank into the bed and into the welcoming dark.

CHAPTER 4

When the world finally drifted back and the nightmares receded, Taylor slowly opened her eyes. Her mouth was dry, tacky, and her head felt as though someone was bashing it with a sledgehammer. It throbbed and ached along with the rest of her body.

She shuddered and moaned when the ache went deeper, pulsing through her bones. She needed to move, couldn't keep still any longer.

A heavy hand settled against her left shoulder, keeping her on her back as she tried to roll onto her side.

What had happened to her?

Her eyes snapped open when it hit her.

Her blurred vision came into focus and she looked at her right arm. Her jacket was gone, and so was the wound. Not even a scar remained. She swallowed and the pain began to recede, drifting away.

A second strong hand came into view.

His fingers brushed the area where the wound had been and she tracked the length of his arm up to his face. He looked worried again. He wouldn't look that way if he knew about her, if he knew what she was.

He couldn't know, and she didn't want to tell him.

Einar smiled at her, not bright or cheerful, but full of warmth.

Taylor reminded herself that he was an angel. That was the only reason he smiled at her that way. It was his duty to be concerned about damsels in distress. It had nothing to do with her being the one in danger.

But then, he had looked at her with such forceful hunger and passion too.

Had that been real?

Taylor stared up into his eyes for a few seconds. When they met hers, she glanced away, her gaze lighting on his shoulder and then taking in his gold-edged brown armour. It didn't hide much of his body. All he wore was a breastplate detailed with dull gold that ended just below his pectorals, vambraces to protect his forearms, greaves to protect his shins, along with his boots, and slats encircling his hips over a dark loincloth.

He looked like a gladiator, with wings.

They were large and furled against his back, as tawny as the rest of him, the long feathers brown but flecked with paler hues of tan and grey. Like an eagle. He had eyes to match that image.

And he was handsome.

There was no denying that.

He was more than handsome. Gorgeous perhaps. Otherworldly. And with muscles to die for. Angels shouldn't have such godly bodies. They only led women into temptation, and she was sure that sort of thing was a sin.

"How long was I out?" she croaked.

He sat on the bed beside her, releasing her shoulder. "Fourteen hours."

Taylor rubbed her throat. Fourteen hours and she still felt as though she needed to sleep it off.

Einar shifted away from her, leaning to his right, and sat back again, offering her a tall glass of water. She took it and he moved towards her. Damn, he smelled good. Earth and fire, with a hint of spice.

"Here, let me help you." His deep voice curled around her, sending that unwanted heat shimmering over her skin again.

Taylor didn't fight him as he took hold of her arm with one hand and placed the other against her shoulder blade, helping her sit up. It took a lot out of her just to shuffle into a comfortable position. When she moved backwards to rest against the pillows, his hand slid down to the small of her back, touching the bare skin above the waist of her jeans.

A shiver raced through her, bringing warmth in its wake.

She stared at him, her thirst forgotten, replaced with something altogether more alarming.

Hunger.

Desire.

Two things she definitely shouldn't be feeling towards an angel.

"Thanks." Taylor shooed him away and sipped the water.

Einar sat beside her again.

The silence was too comfortable.

Taylor looked at her socks, needing something to distract her from the temptation to look at him again. He had taken her boots off. She ran her gaze up her jeans and over her waist. She frowned, glanced around the room, and found what she was looking for on the small wooden cabinet beside the bed.

In a neat row, as though on display, every knife she'd had on her person gleamed under the table lamp.

"I did not want you to hurt yourself. I hope you do not mind that I removed them?" His tone held a note of concern, as if he honestly feared she was going to go off the rails at him again over him removing her weapons.

She supposed she had given him a little hell when he had been trying to help her.

Taylor frowned at the knives, searching for her voice. They were in descending order by size. Either he had been bored while she had been sleeping, or he suffered from obsessive-compulsive disorder.

"Not at all," she murmured, distant as she stared at the knives.

Some of them had been in her jacket, which now lay on a chair across the pale room along with her sword. Others had been sheathed in her boots. And then there were those she'd had strapped against her hips and ribs. The thought of Einar's hands so close to her breasts brought a blush onto her cheeks.

"You do not look well." He leaned closer, filling her senses with his intoxicating masculine scent.

Her blush deepened and her gaze shot to Einar as she touched her blazing cheeks. "I'm fine. Tired, and groggy, and in need of some painkillers, but other than that, I'm good, Romeo."

"I wish you would stop calling me that." His eyes narrowed with his frown and his lips compressed. "I have a name, and I have told it to you."

"Oh." Taylor toyed with the glass of water, suddenly feeling unsure of herself. She didn't want to get on first name terms with him. Danger lay that way. It was better that they remained barely involved in each other's lives, and not calling him by his name was a good method for achieving that, one she had employed many times in the past. "Sure."

"Taylor?" he husked and she cringed.

He had to go and say it, didn't he?

"Yes?" Her gaze remained glued on the glass. She sipped the water, ran her finger around the base, did everything she could to avoid looking at him.

"Do you know much about the breed of demon you encountered last night?"

That seemed like a safe enough question to answer.

"Yes." She risked it and looked at him.

She didn't mean to make eye contact, but hers leaped to his and she found herself staring into them. They mesmerised her as the colours in them shifted and swirled. Not unsettling or scary at all. When his eyes did that, she wanted to look into them forever.

His dark pupils widened, filling his eyes with unmistakable desire, and images of them together on the bed flickered through her mind like old silent movies.

Taylor tried to shun them but they wouldn't go, not while he was looking at her with such hunger and need.

The message in his eyes was clear, written in ten-foot high neon letters that blazed so brightly they blinded her. Men had given her that 'come get me' look plenty of times before, and she had fallen for it a few of those, wanting the passion their eyes had promised. Some of them had even come good on it.

But there was one difference this time.

When she had been promised the ride of her life in the past, it had been by men.

Not angels.

That shocked some sense into her.

She cleared her throat. It wasn't going to happen and her body had better get the message soon. It didn't matter just how good Einar looked, and how easily she could fall into his arms and this bed with him. It was wrong and it would end badly for her.

This was going to be strictly business.

He knew something about the godforsaken scum she had encountered last night. She would bleed him for information on the demons and why they were in her city, deal with them and then dump him. It was the only reason she was going to propose something that would otherwise be the stupidest idea she had ever had.

"I'll tell you about them on one condition." She raised a single finger, held his gaze, and gave him her best seductive smile. "We work together."

He shook his head.

"There is no reason for you to become involved." His deep voice held a note of warning and his face darkened. "I cannot risk you."

Taylor put the glass of water down on the wooden cabinet beside her and glared at him. "I don't need protecting. I can handle myself. I know this city, and the demons that run it, and if you want that information, you're going to have to work with me to get rid of that pain in the arse breed."

Einar's frown deepened and his tone hardened. "Like you handled yourself last night?"

She had been waiting for that one. "You got in the way. I was doing fine until you showed up."

"I was watching you the whole time," he bit out and she wondered whether he knew there was darkness in his eyes now, shadows that an angel shouldn't possess. At least not one of the good ones. His eyes narrowed on her. "You fought well, but he bested you, and you would have been dead had I not intervened."

Taylor sat forward, fury blazing through her and pushing her fatigue to the back of her mind as she realised that he was not only going to deny her help, he was going to belittle her in the process, questioning her strength and skill.

Who the hell did he think he was?

She protected this city with her life and had done for years before he had shown up to play white knight. She would have been fine if she hadn't got in the way. It was his fault the damned demon had managed to get a claw on her.

"Listen." She took hold of his breastplate at the edges near his shoulders and yanked him towards her. His eyes widened as he jerked forwards and then narrowed again. "Either we work together, or I show you up by killing all of that breed before you. I'm pretty sure that'll look bad on your record. A woman beating you to the kill."

Einar calmly removed her hands from his armour and her anger faltered when he didn't let go of them. He held them, gently cradling her fingers in his, and warmth eased up her arms. She snatched her hands back, rattled by how easily he could calm the darkness inside of her.

"I am already in the lead," he said with a twitch of his lips that looked as if it might have been a grin before he had contained it. "I am only after another two. Without your information, it may take time for me to find them. People are in danger while those creatures roam the streets. They have killed many over the past four years. Please. Give me the information I need, Taylor."

Why did he have to keep saying her name? Whenever he said it, rolling it off his tongue in a sensual way, she wanted to melt and give him whatever he was asking for.

She sucked down a deep breath, bolstered her resolve and shook her head. "This is my city. I protect it. You want to get those demons, then you're gonna have to partner with me."

His dark gaze drifted down over her body, a wicked smile tugging at the corners of his mouth.

She could read that look too.

It was more 'coming to get you' than 'come get me' this time but unnerved her just as much.

She wouldn't relent.

If he didn't know about her by now, he would certainly know if he got intimate with her. She didn't want that to happen. She didn't want him to hurt her. Never get involved. Her mother had taught her that and she had obeyed like a good girl, afraid of the consequences if she didn't. She couldn't get involved.

Maybe she should just tell him everything and then leave before things got complicated. She didn't think she could bear someone turning on her, not in the way she was picturing him doing in her head. It would tear her apart inside.

Just as she was resolved to give him the information and leave, he touched her hand and her eyes found his again.

He smiled.

"Deal."

Taylor's stomach dropped two inches.

What had she done?

CHAPTER 5

Einar wasn't sure of the real reason why Taylor had insisted on partnering with him to find the demons, but he was certain that it wasn't just about the fact it was her city and she knew it well. There was something else at play and he wanted to know what it was.

It couldn't be the thing that he had already figured out about her.

In fact, her part-demon blood was the reason he was so surprised that she wanted to work with him.

He had thought that it would be reason enough for her to give him the information he wanted and then leave and never see him again.

Now he had another problem to deal with.

His feelings.

It was wrong of him to agree to working with her, especially given the seriousness of the situation. Taylor was a distraction. It wasn't that he doubted her ability to take care of herself. It was the fact that she was beautiful, alluring, and tempting him even when she wasn't trying to. It was wrong of him to entertain the myriad of devious things that had been flooding his mind all day with images of them together. He hadn't wanted a mortal woman in centuries, and had certainly never lusted after a woman like Taylor.

She drew him to her, a siren both irresistible and deadly, luring him into surrendering to temptation.

He had watched her sleeping, had remained in the suite at the hotel when he should have been out looking for the demons. She hadn't needed him to stay with her. His power had removed all trace of the demon toxin from her blood and she had only needed to recover her strength through sleep.

So why hadn't he been able to leave her side?

He had removed her boots, and then her weapons, and when she hadn't awoken, he had arranged the knives into order. He had inspected her sword. The short silver blade was blessed, which led him to suspect that she was a hunter of sorts. She had said that she protected London and seemed intent on ridding it of a dangerous breed of demon.

Something in common.

They both hunted demons.

He had fought the temptation to brush the black strands of her hair with his fingers, smoothing them against the white pillow, and had yearned for her to open her eyes and look at him, to wake and speak with him. She had stunning deep blue eyes surrounded by long dark lashes that added to her sinful wicked air. He had wanted to see them again and see if he wasn't the only one considering crazy things.

He had gone to his room and tried to sleep, but it had been impossible when he had known that she was lying in the room across the living area of the suite.

She was definitely a distraction.

A beautiful distraction.

She walked beside him, tall, graceful and head held high. As he looked at her, that head slowly turned and her blue eyes met his. The streetlights stole the colour from them, but he could remember it vividly. Not bright like the sky, but deep like the ocean.

"So, how well do you know London?" Taylor led him down another road.

They were heading back towards where they had met the demon last night. She had insisted that they started there. It was a dead end, but for some reason he couldn't help letting her have her own way.

"A little." Around several hundred years' worth of experience but he wasn't about to tell her that.

She was using her knowledge of the city and its demons as her reason for being around him and he didn't want her to leave.

He stopped and watched her walk on ahead, her hips swaying just enough to draw his attention. The dark blue jeans she wore were snug against her bottom and hips, emphasising their shape to him.

What was he doing?

He reasoned with himself that she could fight and that was the only reason he was loath to let her go. If he did, she would go out hunting again and could end up hurt. He didn't want that to happen.

He was doing his duty as an angel by protecting her and keeping her with him.

It had nothing to do with the fact that he was attracted to her.

If anyone discovered that, he would be in serious trouble. Having relations with a mortal was one thing. Falling for a demon was another.

Part-demon.

Einar erased that last thought. Reasoning like that wouldn't stand up in Heaven's Court. If accused of entering into a liaison with a demon, he couldn't retort that she was only part-demon. Her blood made her who she was. Demon or part-demon, it was the same to an angel.

She was off limits.

He realised that she had stopped a short distance away and was standing with her hands on her hips, watching him with a scowl.

He strode towards her and her look softened as he neared, a touch of colour darkening her cheeks. She dropped her gaze and turned her face away. He studied her reaction. It confused him. Several times, she had done something similar. She was bold and brash, had a smart mouth and was prone to fighting him on everything, but there were times when she turned shy and couldn't bring herself to look at him.

Why?

His eyes slowly widened.

Was he the reason she wanted to stay and help him? Was it because she was attracted to him too?

She knew he was an angel. She knew it was forbidden on both sides and that nothing could happen between them.

Didn't she care?

Or was she struggling against desire as much as he was?

Einar followed her as she started moving again, lost in thoughts that plagued him, refused to go away even as he tried to focus on his surroundings and his mission.

They entered the dark park and he came up to walk beside her, remaining close in case any other demons were in the area.

He had been right last night, but on both counts.

They were both heading for trouble.

"Take a look at this." She touched his hand, jolting him out of his thoughts.

Her fingertips brushed his palm and he stared at their joined hands as heat rolled up his arm, had his chest feeling strangely light and his blood rushing in his veins.

Why did something so forbidden have to feel so right?

He lifted his eyes from their hands to her face. Her eyes widened as she looked down at their hands and she quickly released him. She fidgeted with the tears in the sleeve of her biker jacket, looked as if she wanted to say something, and then crouched.

What was she doing?

He frowned down at her. It hit him that they had reached the spot where the demon had turned to ash on him last night.

She touched the dirty patch on the path, fingers traversing it as though she was reading something in the lingering ashes like a psychic reading a palm. A gypsy had done that for him once. She had said that he had a dark future ahead of him. All angels knew they had a dark future. It was called the Apocalypse.

"Picking up anything?" he said in a teasing tone and then reined himself in.

There was no need to encourage her and make her realise that he liked having her around. She would only start torturing him again as she had done last night on the threshold of the hotel suite. The feel of her fingers in his hair, loosening the mousy lengths from his ponytail, had been divine. She had pushed him to the limit with such a simple, small thing, and she had known it. He had seen it in the way she had dropped her hands into her lap and focused there, as though ashamed to have done such a thing with him.

An angel.

And a demon.

It was all very wrong.

"Only that you don't believe in this sort of thing." Taylor's eyes narrowed and she leaned over the charred ground. "It wasn't the Devil."

Tell him something he didn't already know.

"It wasn't the demon's friends either... the two you want. This sort of thing isn't possible for them. This is something else. Judgement by someone else." She looked up at him.

She had his attention now. No more teasing her. She could read something in the dirt beneath her palm. Either that or she knew demons better than he had thought.

Einar crouched beside her and held his hand out over the ash.

Pale light filtered down from his palm and stretched out to cover the entire circle on the pavement. The ash swirled around and then lifted up, drifting towards his palm.

Taylor's soft gasp threatened to shatter his focus.

He concentrated, not allowing her to distract him. It was always difficult to send samples in this manner. If he lost focus, he would have to start all over again, and he didn't want to waste his strength on a second attempt.

The ash reached his hand and disappeared into his palm. When he had collected enough, he fisted his fingers and the light blinked out.

"What did you do?" Her eyes were wide in the low light, fixed on him.

"Magic." He stood and wiped his dirty palm on the rear of his loincloth.

"Liar." She came to stand toe-to-toe with him and stared up into his eyes.

She really was beautiful, especially when she was angry or annoyed. The fire that flashed in her eyes, that set her jaw and made her stand rod-straight, ready for a fight, drew him to her like a moth to flame, and everyone knew how badly that one ended.

He looked at his stained palm. "The lab will be able to analyse the sample. They will contact me when they know something."

"Angels have labs?"

"We have technology far superior to that which the humans use. It makes life easier when we can ascertain the type of demon responsible and check the database to see their habits. It is far quicker to catch them then." He nearly smiled when she looked disappointed, as though he had just told her that Santa Claus didn't exist. "What, you think that angels are all-powerful and have the knowledge of the ages stuffed into our heads? That we see everything and know everything, and can find a wrongdoer at the drop of a pin?"

"Next you'll be telling me you don't dance on the heads of those pins." She raked her gaze over him, a single dark eyebrow rising as she did so. Her voice dropped to a sultry whisper. "Although you're a little big for pinhead dancing."

His blood burned at the sight of the desire written plainly across her face and in her tone. He fought the temptation to show her just how big he was, and just what sort of dance with her he had in mind, and won this time.

Her blue gaze met his in the dim night.

"There are some things I do not have to be an angel to see." He reached out to touch her cheek but she backed away and busied herself with looking at the charred circle on the path.

He curled his fingers into a fist and sighed. Maybe he was wrong about her and she was only teasing him.

He closed his eyes.

Maybe he shouldn't care.

Maybe he should call it quits now and leave her before things got even more complicated.

"Listen, Taylor—" Einar froze, his senses blaring danger. She turned towards him, her eyes wide and expectant. "Get down!"

He grabbed her, wrapped her in his arms, and hit the ground.

CHAPTER 6

Taylor's breath left her on impact with the hard cold grass. Einar's weight pressed down on her, both delicious and painful. His thick toned left thigh wedged between her legs, against the apex of them, and her face was squashed against his shoulder. He had his hands over her head, cradling her to him, and everything was very dark.

She realised that his wings were covering her.

And that they weren't alone.

There had been a loud bang when he had grabbed her, and then a bright flash.

The smell of burning sulphur filled her nostrils, acrid and choking. Something straight out of Hell had come to pay her a visit, and she wasn't one to disappoint her guests.

The moment Einar moved off her, she was on her feet.

She reached over her head to grab her blade and growled when she remembered that she had let Einar convince her to leave it in his hotel suite, so they didn't look conspicuous when walking the streets of London. She had never had a problem with carrying the blade before. Normally she wore it strapped to her back beneath her jacket. No one saw it there.

Why had she been so weak and let Einar have his way?

She should have told him to go to Hell and taken the weapon anyway.

She glared at him when he stepped in front of her, shielding her as he had last night, as though she needed his protection. Her gaze drifted down to his bare waist and the sword hanging beside his left hip.

Well, he could make up for leading her into this situation poorly armed.

Taylor raced past him, grabbing his sword on the way, and ignored his shout of protest.

She narrowed her eyes on the demon in front of her. Huge, horned, black as sin, and belching smoke and flames in the darkness.

Had someone released this beast to make her and Einar think it had been the one to kill the demon last night?

They were underestimating her.

She knew her demons and this one was nothing more than a heavy hand, and it certainly didn't have the ability to make a demon disappear so neatly. If it killed her, she would be a long dark bloody streak on ground pockmarked by huge craters.

Subtlety wasn't in its repertoire.

As if to prove her point, it opened its mouth and released a massive fireball that shot towards her.

Taylor dived to her left, narrowly avoiding the blast, feeling the heat of it scalding her boots.

The world shook when the flaming missile carved up the dirt and a shockwave caught her. She slammed into the ground, rolled onto her feet and kept running at the demon.

A cursory glance around the poorly lit park revealed that Einar was gone.

She refused to believe that the demon could have got him so easily but the thought that it might have distracted her enough that she almost didn't notice the second fireball.

It flashed past her, so hot and close that if she hadn't been wearing her thick leather jacket, her arm would have been toast. She flinched and doubled her pace, coming around the demon.

It moved slowly, belching fiery missiles at her, and she managed to get ahead of them.

Taylor changed course and headed straight for the demon, raising her borrowed sword at the same time. It was heavier than her own one but she could handle it. Maybe.

She yelled and swiped at the demon, barely reaching its knees. It growled, exposing long black teeth that could easily crush her head. In fact, it could probably eat her in one bite.

It didn't stop her. She used her fear as fuel to keep her going. It was kill or be killed, and she wasn't going to die here tonight.

The demon's bright flaming eyes tracked her as it lumbered backwards, avoiding her blows. Smoke billowed from between its jagged teeth, the occasional spark joining it and dancing around in the night like a firefly before dying away. She attacked again, hacking the demon's black hand and dodging when it swiped at her as though she was nothing more than an insect bothering it.

Where the hell was Einar?

She glanced around again at the empty park.

Had he done a runner?

Was he going to let her fight alone just because she had taken his sword? Surely, he had other weapons at his disposal? He had powers that he could probably use in a fight somehow. She didn't. It was only fair that she got to have the sword.

The demon roared and a stream of fire shot towards her from its mouth. She leaped, rolled and dived, avoiding becoming nothing more than a dark line on the dirt. She was seriously not going to die here tonight.

This demon was.

Taylor yelled back at the demon and swung her blade.

A bright white light shot down over the demon, blinding her, and then a shockwave hurled her backwards.

She hit the wet grass hard, skidding along it and grimacing as she lost her grip on the sword. When she came to a halt, she immediately looked towards the demon and stilled.

A shaft of light encased it, reaching high into the sky like a searchlight beam. She followed it upwards and stopped when she saw Einar. He hovered far above the ground, steadily beating his wings, the white light glinting off his dark armour and highlighting him.

When she had figured he had powers he could use to fight the demon, she hadn't quite been imagining this.

She pushed onto her feet, dusted the blades of grass and globs of mud off her dark jeans, and stomped towards the long sword where it lay on the grass. She picked it up and cautiously approached the beam of light and the demon frozen within it.

Looked up at Einar.

He slowly descended, a somewhat smug look on his face.

Show off.

He landed in front of her, his expression fixed in a way that made her think he wanted praise for what he had done. Okay, it was impressive, but she wasn't about to let him know that. She wasn't into rubbing men's egos.

"What the hell was that about? You could have hit me too!" She prodded him in the breastplate with the tip of the sword and he frowned at her. She frowned right back at him. "You threw me halfway to Hell with that stupid trick."

"You were in the way." He calmly brushed the sword aside with the back of his hand.

"What, so you thought you'd take a shot and hope you'd only toss me through the air and not trap me too?" She planted her free hand against her hip, scowled at him and waited to hear his excuse.

"What else was I supposed to do?" He hiked his broad shoulders in a shrug and furled his tawny wings against his back. "You *were* in the way. Besides, I have done this enough times to be accurate in my aim."

"Accurate my arse." She rubbed her backside. It still ached from the impact.

"Are you hurt?" The anger in his expression melted away to reveal concern.

Damn he looked good when he was worried about her.

She couldn't be mad at him when he was looking as sweet as a puppy dog. She blamed her human blood for such a weakness. If she had been all demon, she would have been able to keep hold of her fury just as she wanted to.

But then, if she had been all demon, Einar would have let her die last night, and he certainly wouldn't be looking at her with such warmth.

"I'll live," she muttered and shifted her attention to the black demon in the shaft of light, hoping it would move Einar's focus there too. "What'll happen to it?"

Einar waved his hand and the demon began to ascend towards the dark sky. Her gaze tracked it, watching it getting smaller and smaller, and then it disappeared from view and the beam of light flickered and died, leaving the park in near-darkness again.

"We will question it. It may provide us with answers." He turned towards her and held out his hand.

Taylor stared at it.

He cleared his throat, rolled his fingers and gave her an unimpressed look. She jolted when she remembered that she had his sword. She handed it to him. He shook his head and held his other hand out, as though he wanted something else.

She swallowed.

Her hand?

She couldn't do that.

"I just want to heal you," he whispered, sultry and low, in a way that conjured wicked thoughts and said he wanted to do a lot more than heal her with his touch.

"I'm fine." She patted herself all over, smiling the whole time, hoping to emphasise her point so he wouldn't try to touch her. She wasn't sure that she would be able to resist him if he did. She had to think of some way to distract him from the fact that he had hurt her. "So... labs, interrogation teams, what else is new in Heaven?"

He raised a single dark eyebrow and took his hand back. He slid the sword into the sheath hanging from his waist and shrugged as it clanked against the pointed slats of the armour around his hips.

"Nothing. We have been working this way for centuries." He checked her over again, looking as if he was going to make another attempt to heal her.

She raked her gaze over him, using him as a distraction now. "What sort of angel are you exactly? The last one I met had white wings. I don't remember meeting your sort before."

He gave her a hard look. Not happy about the way she was talking about him? He was going to have to get used to it. It was the easiest way of making him maintain his distance.

"I am a hunter." He adjusted his sword and settled his hand on the hilt.

"Makes sense." Taylor couldn't resist the opportunity to cast her eye over him again.

He looked as though he could handle hunting. Bronzed skin stretched taut over powerful muscles, and the weapon hanging at his waist could slay her any day of the week. She coughed to clear her throat and chase such thoughts away. She was not going to fall for an angel. Her mother would laugh in her grave.

"I'm a hunter too." If she'd had a blade on her, she would have twirled it, showing off her skills.

Einar had made her leave all her toys at his place though.

He didn't say anything, just lifted his head towards the sky, stood silent and pensive for so long she wondered if something was wrong with him.

He dropped his gaze to her. "Where is Cloud Nine?"

Her eyebrows rose.

She saw a chance to tease him and took it. "You're an angel. I thought you'd be able to answer that one. I've never been on cloud nine myself, but I've heard good things about it. I bet it's pretty crowded though, unless it's really big. Do angels get to go to cloud nine too?"

He didn't look impressed. He was quiet again, as pensive as before, and then nodded as though agreeing with something. Her? She looked up at the night sky. Or someone else?

"It is a club, apparently, in this city. The demon we apprehended has pointed us in the direction of it. Do you know where it is?" His deep luscious voice made her eyes half-close.

She nodded absently and then her eyes shot wide when she remembered exactly what sort of club Cloud Nine was. "Are you sure you want to go there? I mean, it's an—"

"Exotic club?" He smiled, bright and dazzling. "I got the memo."

"Where, in your head?" She looked around his ears for a sign of anything that could serve as a communications device.

He nodded. "Of course. Where else would I receive orders?"

The way he said that made it sound as though it was perfectly normal to have voices talking to you in your head, telling you to do things. As far as she knew, that sort of thing usually got you committed.

"Whatever you say." She tugged her leather jacket closed over her chest and started towards the park exit.

Cloud Nine had a reputation as a sleaze pit and for a good reason. It was the sort of club a human went to when they wanted to get off their face and do things without any strings attached and no consequences.

Unfortunately for the mortals, half of the patrons were of the demonic variety, and some of them had dangerous habits.

The sort that could get angels asking questions and hunting them down.

He had said that he was after the three demons because they had worked with an angel to kill over one hundred humans, and he needed to know why.

Did it have something to do with what happened at Cloud Nine?

She shook that theory away.

Cloud Nine had a reputation, but not for murder.

There had only ever been the occasional accident.

If it had been the scene of so much death, she would have heard about it. Besides, she was sure that the boss wouldn't condone such things. They had always kept a strict eye on the demons who frequented the club, and most of them obeyed the rules. The boss dealt with those who didn't in a way that was a warning to the rest and kept them in line.

It had to be something else that had killed the humans, or at least somewhere else.

"You are very quiet." Einar's voice drifted into her thoughts and she made a small noise of agreement. "Thinking?"

"About Cloud Nine. I get the why, but I'm not sure it's right." She looked across at him.

He strode beside her, tall, dark and too handsome for his own good, especially when he smiled at her.

There was something mischievous about it this time.

"You can tell me all about it while we are en route."

Before she could agree, he had swept her into his arms and had kicked off, beating his broad tawny wings and lifting them both into the air. She grabbed him around the neck and curled up.

"Put me down. I thought we went through this last night? I am not flying with you." She beat his chest with one hand and clung fiercely to him with the other.

The ground drifted farther and farther away and her stomach turned.

"I will not drop you. There is no reason to fear." His grip on her tightened, offering comfort she refused to accept.

There was every reason. "If God had wanted me to fly, he would have given *me* wings."

"Well, he gave me wings, so we are flying. It is far quicker and I am tired of walking." The stubborn set of his jaw told Taylor that she wasn't going to get her way this time either.

The world rushed by below. She baulked and hid her face in his neck. It wasn't strong or very like her, but she couldn't face seeing how high she was and how easily she could fall.

Einar's strong grip on her ribs and knees said that she couldn't fall that easily. It had taken her beating him up last night to get him to let her go. He wouldn't drop her. She trusted him that much.

"You do need to direct me," he said in a loud voice over the sound of the wind.

She emerged from her hiding place, steeled her stomach and looked around, trying to make sense of the alien world below her. The BT tower glowed in the distance like a beacon. She pointed towards it. Once they were there, she would be able to direct him.

"Do you think Cloud Nine is the sort of place our demons might have contacts?" He twisted in the air, heading towards the tower.

She looked up at him. His profile was a far better distraction than hiding against his chest. She put it to memory. The straight line of his nose, the sharp edge to his dark eyes, and the chiselled stroke of his jaw. The wind ruffled his short ponytail, freeing strands that whipped against his face. She held her own long black hair with one hand and on to him with the other.

"They might. We don't often get their sort around here though. They tend to keep a low profile." She found herself shouting too, even though she was sure there wasn't any need to. Both of them had superior hearing thanks to their breeding. "Normally I hunt the boring type that just keels over and dies the moment I look at it. I prefer a man with a bit of spunk and fight."

His gaze snapped to meet hers, full of questions. Her cheeks burned. There was no way she had meant him. Not a chance in Hell. Her heart trembled in her throat and her palms sweated. She didn't. She couldn't.

Einar swooped lower and she took to directing him towards the club, thankful for the distraction. She had to get her head on straight. All she had done since meeting him was flirt with him and she had promised herself that she wouldn't get involved.

No matter how much she wanted to.

They landed in the alley outside the club. The neon sign above the entrance was dark. The streets were empty. Einar set her down and she went to the black doors, gripped the handles and rattled them. Locked.

"Guess we'll have to come back tomorrow." Taylor struggled to hold his gaze.

She should have said that he would have to come back tomorrow, should have made up some excuse about having something else to do like washing her hair and left him to find his demons alone. It would have been the most sensible course of action. But then, she hadn't done anything that could be considered sensible from the moment she had met him. He had turned her world upside down and her with it.

She moved back a step, placing more distance between them. "I mean, you'll have to come back."

She turned to leave but he caught her arm. She looked down at his hand, at his fingers engulfing her slender wrist, and then up into his eyes.

"I thought we were partners?" His dark eyes searched hers, his eyebrows knitted hard above them.

She cursed that word.

Partners.

Perhaps they were, but not the sort that she wanted. That was something they could never be. It was too complicated and it would never work.

If Heaven found out that he had worked with her, or healed her, or anything about them, then they would punish him. At least she only had to answer to herself. It wasn't like that for him though, and she didn't want to be responsible for getting him kicked out of his job and his home.

And she didn't want him to hate her when he realised what she was.

"I really should leave." She tried to take her hand back but he wouldn't let it go.

"Why?" Einar stepped up to her, so close that his hip brushed hers, and she trembled at the feel of him.

She couldn't say the answers that came to her. Her voice wouldn't work.

Because it was forbidden.

Because she wanted so much more than just helping him find some damned demons.

Because he was going to break her heart.

Because he would hate her.

Instead, she stood there, staring into his eyes, losing a battle she didn't have the heart to fight.

"No reason," she said and he released her hand. She managed to fake a wicked smile even though she ached inside. "I guess we should stick together for now then, Partner."

She traced her fingers along the top of his breastplate, following the gold edging around the moulded dark brown leather, and his gaze tracked them.

It hurt to flirt with him, but using it to cover her feelings was far easier than facing her fear by telling him what was on her mind and confessing that she was the sort of thing he was out to kill.

Einar swept her into his arms again and took flight with her. She looped her arms around his neck and rested her head on his shoulder as her thoughts weighed her down, silencing her tongue.

He held her closer, as though he had sensed her need for reassurance, and his cheek brushed her forehead. He remained there, his warm skin touching hers, and she realised something.

She wasn't the only one battling their feelings and desire.

But she would be the one to surrender to them.

CHAPTER 7

Einar held the door to the hotel suite open for Taylor. She passed him and flicked on the lights. The living area between the two bedrooms held her attention in a way that wasn't natural.

There wasn't much to look at. Two gilt-framed cream couches facing each other across a wooden coffee table and a flat screen TV on a side cupboard between the two tall windows opposite the door.

Was she avoiding looking at him?

Angels had acute senses. He could feel her fear and desire. They mirrored his own feelings so perfectly that he hadn't noticed them as hers at first. It didn't help that she insisted on flirting with him one moment and trying to push him away the next.

Was she as confused about this as he was?

Both of them knew it wasn't right, even if it did feel as though it was.

Taylor walked to the door of the second bedroom.

Einar watched her backside sway, appreciated the hell out of her curves as he raked his gaze over them. She was more than tempting. He wanted her without a doubt, but no good would come of it. She knew what he was, and why they couldn't do this.

She stopped at the door and looked back at him. Her black hair swept over her shoulder in a graceful wave, blending into her leather jacket, and her blue eyes held his, mesmerising him.

He went to her without thinking, his feet moving of their own volition, carrying him towards the one thing he shouldn't want but the one thing he couldn't resist.

Taylor.

She was beautiful.

And he was starting not to care about her blood or what she was, because all of that made her into the woman standing before him. This beautiful woman with so much passion and fear in her eyes, so much conflict that he wanted to touch her cheek and kiss her, and show her that it didn't matter where they had come from in life.

It only mattered that they were falling for each other.

He almost laughed at himself.

What foolish thoughts were those?

She flirted with him but that didn't mean she actually wanted him. For all he knew, this was some devious demonic game to her, a challenge to make an angel fall.

He stopped close beside her, staring deep into her eyes and trying to decipher her true feelings. A sparkle of tears wet her lashes and for a flicker of a moment, pure fear replaced any trace of desire in her eyes.

No.

This wasn't a game.

This was real, for both of them. They were both scared. She was just fighting it better than he was.

He had given up the moment he had touched her, and she had touched him, last night.

Taylor stepped up to him, pressed her hand against the breastplate of his armour, and tiptoed.

He couldn't move as she brought her mouth towards his, her eyes closing. Froze solid when she kissed him.

It was soft, tentative, and mind-blowing.

Any hint of reservation and restraint he had shattered in an instant.

He started to kiss her but she pulled away and took a step backwards towards the open door of her room, her fingers trailing down his breastplate as she smiled.

"Thanks for the date, Romeo." She turned, stepped into her room and closed the door on him.

Einar stood staring at the white panels, breathing hard and struggling to regain control as the need she had ignited in him raged just below the surface, fighting to get free.

Was she trying to break him? Was she just toying with him or was she serious?

He fought the urge to kick her door down and ask her, and kiss her, and make love with her. Every inch of him tightened at the thought of burying himself in her sweet body and slaking his thirst for her.

He pressed his hand against the door and drew deep breaths, wrestling for some sort of command over his feelings.

She moved around on the other side, coming closer one moment and drifting away the next. He listened, trying to convince himself to turn around and go to his room. It was impossible with the taste of her on his tongue and the memory of how good her mouth had felt against his rampaging through his mind.

He didn't care if it was real or not.

He didn't care about the consequences.

Einar kicked the door and it burst open, slamming against the wall on the other side.

Taylor gasped and his gaze sought her out.

She stood at the foot of the white double bed, clutching her black top to her bare breasts, her blue eyes wide.

His chest heaved as he stared at her, as he raked his gaze down over her wicked curves, his heart pounding faster at the sight of her.

He crossed the room in two strides and pulled her into his arms.

She dropped her top and pressed her hands against his breastplate when he dipped his head and captured her lips. He crushed them with a passionate kiss, holding nothing back as his tongue delved beyond the barrier of her teeth to tangle with hers.

She moaned, leaned into him, and slid her hands up, settling her arms around his neck. Tingles cascaded down his spine as she buried her fingers into his hair.

It didn't matter that it was forbidden.

It only mattered that they wanted this, needed this, and had feelings for each other.

To Hell with it.

Taylor gasped again as he scooped her up, his mouth still playing sensually with hers, and kneeled on the bed. She giggled when he laid her down on the soft white bedclothes and covered her.

He relinquished her lips and looked down at his armour.

She was right.

It had to go.

He undid the leather strap over his right shoulder with one hand and stilled as she unbuckled the other, her actions slow and tantalising, teasing his senses. She brushed her fingers over his bare skin and swept them down the solid armour to his side, and all he could do was watch as she undid the side strap on his left and then dealt with the one on his right.

Her soft pink tongue swept across her lips as she removed the breastplate and her gaze fell to his body. She tossed the armour to one side and her eyes darkened when she ran both of her hands over his bare chest. He tensed beneath her delicious touch and she moaned.

"Like a god," she whispered and traced the lines of his abdomen and chest, her gaze burning into his body, leaving a fiery trail.

He dragged his eyes away from hers and held his own groan at bay when he saw her bare full breasts, their dusky peaks taut and begging for attention. He wanted her. It screamed in every fibre of his body, a hunger so intense that it felt as though he would die if he couldn't satisfy it.

There was something he needed to do first.

Einar focused hard.

She frowned. "What's the ma—"

He pressed his finger to her lips and concentrated.

Her eyes widened when his wings began to shrink into his back.

When they had disappeared, he stood and removed the back plate of his armour. She sat up on the edge of the bed, her eyes on him, following his every move as he undressed. He unbuckled his greaves and boots, and kicked them off. When he went to do the same with the vambraces protecting his forearms, she stopped him.

Einar stilled again and let her have her way. It was far more enjoyable when she undressed him after all.

She ran her hands over his left one, her movements leisurely as she turned it so his palm was face up. He swallowed when she carefully undid each buckle on the armguard, her fingers lightly teasing the patch of skin that action exposed. When she reached the final buckle and had dealt with it, she slowly removed the vambrace and set it down on the bed beside her. He thought she was done with him, that she would move on to his other arm without hesitation.

She swept her hands up the thick toned length of his forearm instead and her thumbs caressed the soft skin on the inside of his elbow.

He stared into her eyes when she held his elbow with one hand and brought her other back down to his hand. She lured it towards her and he swallowed again, his mouth drying out as she moulded his fingers around her right breast. His eyes slipped shut and he palmed her, loving the warm weighted feel of it in his hand.

He was so lost in playing with it that he didn't notice she had finished with his other vambrace until her hands skimmed across his waist and she started on his sword belt and the armour that protected his hips.

Einar froze then, every sense he had focusing on her hands and the way they caressed and teased as she removed his sword and then unbuckled the armour, leaving him in only his dark loincloth.

Taylor paused too and looked up at him. Her fingers shook against his waist. Something wasn't right. He could feel fear in her, drumming in her blood, but desire was there too, the same unrelenting beat that pounded inside him, driving him onwards.

His gaze met hers.

"Tell me this isn't wrong," she whispered.

Einar cupped her cheek, swept his hand down to her jaw, leaned over and kissed her.

"This isn't wrong." He peppered her mouth with kisses, short bursts that drove him wild, increasing his desire for her.

It chased away her fear too, had her arching towards him for more, seeking another kiss whenever he broke away from her lips. She leaned back and he followed her, covering her body with his and losing himself in the sensual way her tongue teased his.

Taylor rolled him over, settling her legs on either side of his hips, and stole command of the kiss. He let her have it, too mesmerised by the feel of her bare breasts pressing against his chest to care. She shivered when he wrapped his arms around her and ran his hands down her back, exploring everything he could reach. Her silky skin was warm beneath his fingers, tantalising his senses.

She felt so good against him, in his arms.

He groaned into her mouth when she wriggled her hips, grinding them against his erection. She sighed and did it again. Her tight jeans weren't what he wanted to feel. He wanted to feel her. She squeaked when he sat up, lifting her off him, and set her down on the floor at the foot of the bed.

A naughty smile curved her lips when he hastily undid her belt, unzipped her jeans and pushed them down her legs. She kicked her boots off and then her jeans, and shoved his shoulder.

Hard.

He fell back onto the bed and stretched his arms out at his sides, savouring the view. She was divine before him, wearing only black panties, a real goddess.

He bit his lip when she mounted the bed and then him, coming to sit back astride his hips.

A momentary flicker of doubt crossed her eyes and his mind too. She had asked him to reassure her that this wasn't wrong. It didn't feel wrong, so how could it be?

Wanting to reassure her again, he took hold of her hand and pulled her back to him. Her mouth fused with his, her kiss fierce and wild in a heartbeat. He could kiss her like this for hours, days, and never grow bored.

Taylor had other ideas. She shifted against him, rubbing his cock, distracting him with wanting other things and tearing a moan from his lips.

He slid his hands down her sides, smiling against her mouth when she giggled, and cupped her backside.

This couldn't be wrong.

He didn't care that there were laws against it.

He wanted her and he was going to have her.

She moved backwards, kissing down his bare chest, tongue swirling around his left nipple, lips pressing against his stomach. He closed his eyes and leaned his head back into the bed. It felt far too good to be wrong.

His eyes shot open when she tugged at his loincloth and muttered a ripe curse. Unable to undo it, she took to rubbing him through the material, driving him insane. He needed to feel her hand on him.

It wasn't right to use his powers for such a thing, but right and wrong meant nothing to him in this moment.

He focused.

In the blink of an eye, the remaining barriers between them were gone. Both his loincloth and her underwear. A flicker of surprise danced across her face and then she grinned, lowered her head and licked the length of his cock.

He hissed out his breath and clutched at the white bedclothes.

It had been too long since he had been with someone.

She licked him again, caressing the sensitive head with her tongue, and stroking the shaft with her fingers. He shuddered and moaned, fisting the sheets and fighting for restraint. It was impossible. He had to have her.

He grabbed her hand and yanked her up the length of his body, tearing a gasp from her. Her surprise faded as she lay on top of him and glanced at his hand where it held her wrist, his fingers locked tightly around it.

Her pupils dilated. A pulse of desire swept through him. She liked it rough.

He groaned.

She was going to be his undoing.

She moaned quietly when he tightened his grip on her wrist to gauge whether he was right about her. Her teeth teased her lower lip, that flare of desire in her eyes growing stronger. He dragged her high up his body, so he could kiss her and nibble that lip for her. Her teeth clashed with his as she fought him for dominance but she wouldn't get her way this time.

Wicked thoughts spiralled through his mind, scenarios that he hadn't considered before.

She was strong. She could probably handle him as no other woman had before her.

He rolled them over and nestled between her sweet thighs, his hard length pressed against her mound. He thrust and she groaned into his mouth and buried her fingers in his hair, twisting the lengths tightly around them and holding him to her. He grabbed her hip, fingers pressing in, and held her as he thrust again, hungry to gain some satisfaction.

"Einar," she whispered into his mouth, hot and sultry, full of the need raging inside him.

The sound of her saying his name in such a heated manner branded itself on his mind. It was the first time it had left her lips and he would never forget the way she had said it with so much passion and desire.

She uttered it again when he slid a hand between them and teased her with his fingers, circling her swollen arousal. He groaned and devoured her mouth, tongue tracing her lips, teeth, every part of her. Her grip on him tightened when he delved his fingers lower, almost dipping them into her warm core. His cock ached and kicked. He wanted to be sheathed in there, encased in her heat and joined with her.

He took hold of his shaft and eased the tip of it down, rubbing the length of her with it and tugging another low, sultry moan from her. She grasped his shoulder with one hand and his hair with the other, holding him close to her as he teased her. She groaned and shook, rocked her hips up to meet him.

Tensed and froze.

He drew back, his gaze meeting hers. He knew what she needed to hear. He held her gaze, letting her see the truth of it in his eyes, and stroked the rogue strands of her black hair from her face.

"This isn't wrong, Taylor. It cannot be... not when it feels so right."

She nodded but a trace of fear lingered. It lingered inside him too, but he wasn't going to let it stop him. This had to happen between them. There was no way he could stop himself now. He could see there was no way she wanted to stop either. She wanted this too. She wanted him as badly as he needed her.

Her eyes widened slightly when he gently eased his cock into her body, doing it slowly to savour the feeling of their first joining. She was hot and tight around him, so good that he struggled not to climax. It had been too long. He couldn't promise her fireworks. At least not this time.

He groaned when his pelvis brushed hers, his body buried deep inside her, one with her, and continued to hold her gaze, wanting her to see that she wasn't the only one who was a little afraid of this. They were in this together now. Whatever the consequences were, they wouldn't face them alone.

The fear in her eyes faded when he drew back and thrust into her again, long deep strokes that buried him to the hilt. Her lips parted and she dragged him down to her, claimed his mouth and kissed him roughly, her breathing choppy against his face.

She clung to him and moaned as she raised her hips and he plunged into her again, deeper this time. It tore an answering groan from his throat and he grasped her hip, holding her in place as he pumped her, harder and faster, until she was moaning with each deep thrust of his cock.

She tensed around him and he trembled, close to the edge and desperate to hold off so he wouldn't disappoint her. Her nails scored lines down his biceps, fingers tangled in his hair, and teeth nibbled his lip, pushing him to the edge. He groaned and thrust harder, letting go of his restraint. His reward was a louder moan from her, one that filled the room with the delicious sound, and he slid a hand beneath her back and held her to him.

Taylor tipped her head back and dug her fingers into his arm and neck. "More... Einar."

The hunger she said his name with drove him on. He buried his face in her throat, kissing and licking it, biting her collarbone and eliciting a sexy giggle from her. He groaned and thrust harder, unleashing more of his strength on her. She took it all. She took everything he threw at her and it only made her moan louder.

She rocked her hips against his, clenching and unclenching around his length, and he couldn't take any more.

He shuddered to a halt inside her, throbbing and spilling his seed as he breathed hard against her neck, his moans staccato as his heart thundered against his chest. Hers beat in response, just as fast as she wriggled, writhing beneath him, seeking her release.

Einar shifted aside, keeping his cock in her and shallowly pumping her as he teased her aroused nub, swirling his fingers around it. She moaned and he watched the ripples of pleasure crossing her face as she alternated between frowning and sighing. She gasped and jerked against him, her mouth falling open and her eyebrows knitting tightly as her body throbbed around his, milking his softening length, and he knew he would never regret this moment with her, or any that came after.

Her expression went slack as she relaxed into the bed and then she opened her eyes and smiled right into his.

He would never regret anything when it came to her.

His beautiful demoness.

CHAPTER 8

The club was open. Taylor could hear it from up the street. The heavy pounding beat of the music and the chatter of the patrons waiting outside filled the night air. She rounded the corner with Einar. He had changed his appearance again. Not that it ever changed to her. Whatever glamour he used, she would always see right through it to the truth, and so would any demon in the club.

The queue curled out from the entrance and almost around the corner. She ignored the dirty looks that the barely-dressed women and men tossed at her as she strode towards the entrance.

The demon on the door froze when he caught sight of them.

He frowned, lowered the clipboard in his hand to his side, and brought his other hand to his mouth. The hiss of static joined the pounding of the music and the man's expression switched to one of concentration.

He was telling on them.

Taylor sidled up to him, her smile sweet and charming, but her body coiled tight and ready for a fight. Her sword was beneath her leather jacket tonight, strapped to her back where it belonged. It had only taken mentioning how many demons were employed at the club and frequented it to convince Einar to let her come to the party armed and dangerous.

The man towered over her, three hundred plus pounds of muscle wrapped in tight black clothing and topped off with a shaven head. Most people would fear him, but not her. He was just a big obstacle blocking her path and she could easily move him.

Einar hung back.

Taylor was glad that he was giving her room to work her magic on the bouncer and not crowding her, but another part of her had secretly hoped he would remain close and be jealous about the fact that she was going to flirt with the demon. She wasn't doing it to make Einar jealous, but it would be a nice bonus, one that would go a hell of a long way towards making her feel fabulous, and maybe a little less awkward and nervous about what they had done.

"Hi," she whispered and took hold of the man's large hand, bringing the walkie-talkie away from his mouth.

His pale eyes fixed on hers. If she didn't know better, she would have said that he was a vampire with those eyes. He didn't have the class though, or the looks. This man was barely more intelligent than the demon they had fought last night. Another heavy hand.

"Are we on the list?" She smiled, released his hand and angled her head so she could see the clipboard.

Demons could just walk into Cloud Nine, and sometimes she did in order to meet a contact, speak to the boss, or bleed someone for information. She had never come here on a weekend though, when it was so busy, and she wasn't sure what awaited her on the other side. Normally she got here early, got her business over with, and left before the crowds came and started their masquerade.

"Maybe you are, but he isn't." The man nodded over her head.

Taylor could feel Einar there, a glowering dark presence that had an edge to it she hadn't noticed about him before. As sharp as a razorblade. Einar wasn't happy. His gaze drilled into her and she resisted the temptation to turn and see what he looked like, and whether this black malevolence was the jealousy she had been hoping to provoke.

If it was, then she was playing with fire.

She hadn't expected Einar would bear such darkness inside him, but every sense in her was firing and telling her that she was in danger.

Could angels be violent?

She hadn't witnessed it before, and Einar had fought calmly both times they had battled demons together, but she felt it in him, held just below the surface, barely restrained.

If she made a wrong move, one he didn't approve of, would he kill this demon in front of all these people? Would he reveal to them what he was?

It didn't sound like the sort of thing an angel should do.

But then, neither was sleeping with a demon.

Her heart skipped a beat at the memory.

Einar was right. Something that felt so good couldn't be wrong.

She wasn't sure he would be saying that if he knew what she was though, and she was convinced that he didn't. She was convinced that his words last night had been because he had thought that she was a mortal afraid of sleeping with an angel.

"Come on, I just need to ask your boss a few questions." She flashed her smile again but didn't flirt with the bouncer as she had intended. She didn't want to push Einar too far. She had him jealous now, and had no desire to see him furious. She waved a hand at the walkie-talkie the man held. "So, call your boss, and tell them Taylor needs a word, and let us in."

"Nu-uh. His kind are bad for business."

Taylor sighed, grabbed the man's hand and forced it to his mouth. "Listen. Either you call your boss, or the guy you're referring to is going to get really cranky. He's already sent someone up north for a little interrogation time, so I would do as I say."

The demon still hesitated.

The people in the queue near her stared.

There was a crackle and hiss, and then a female voice came over the radio.

"Let them in."

Taylor looked up at the CCTV camera mounted on the wall above the dark double doors behind the bouncer. She winked at it and released him.

When she turned to face Einar, he looked darker than she had expected.

Shadows shrouded his face and clung to his body, as though he was made from the darkness itself. His eyes burned with bright gold flames in the dimly lit street, fixed over her head on the bouncer. The man was already going about his business again as though nothing had happened.

She walked over to Einar but he didn't look at her.

She placed her hand on his chest, wishing she could touch his body rather than the hard, cold breastplate of his armour. His gaze finally dropped to hers but the gold in it still shifted and swirled, creating mesmerising patterns around his narrowed pupils.

She couldn't find her voice to ask if he was alright, not when he placed his hand over hers and held it to his chest. He gripped it tightly, with the same strength he had shown her last night in the bedroom, possessive and unrelenting. She stared into his eyes, wanting the tension between them to disappear.

His pupils widened and the gold flecks settled, only moving slightly as his eyes darted between hers. His lips parted and hers followed suit.

She wanted to kiss him when he looked at her like that.

Did he want to kiss her too?

They hadn't talked about what had happened between them. Neither of them had mentioned anything about it since waking tangled in each other's arms this afternoon. She wanted to discuss what had happened, but she was afraid that he would have changed his mind and would see their moment of passion together as a moment of sheer madness now.

But he was holding her hand, and he looked as though he wanted to kiss her, in public, in front of another demon.

She wished he would.

A kiss from him here, now, would chase away all her fears and quieten the voice at the back of her mind that was constantly telling her she had made a mistake by getting intimate with him.

He was in her heart now, and he could easily break it.

When he didn't make a move, her shoulders sagged and she turned away so he didn't see her disappointment, nodding towards the club.

"We should go in before the boss changes her mind. She can be quite fickle." She walked away from him, heading for the black double doors and trying to ignore the ache behind her sternum.

The mountain of bouncer unhooked the velvet rope and shifted aside to make room for her. She turned back at the door and looked at Einar. He still stood across the alley, shadowed and menacing.

Was she making a mistake by bringing him to Cloud Nine?

She wasn't afraid that the sort of things that happened in the club could corrupt him. She was afraid that he would cause a scene and get her banned. Cloud Nine was her best source of information when she was hunting unfamiliar demon species. She needed it right now, and after Einar was gone.

Her chest throbbed dully at the thought of him leaving. A venomous voice in her heart said that he would.

An angel could never love a demon.

Had she made a terrible mistake by sleeping with him?

Einar left the shadows and strode over to her, muscles shifting in entrancing ways with each step, reminding her of just how good he had looked naked and just how much she still wanted him.

Perhaps there were other reasons it was a mistake to bring him to Cloud Nine.

Seeing all the people in the club having a good time, letting go of their inhibitions and embracing a world without consequence, a night of madness and fun, and indulging in their fantasies, would push her to the limit with Einar.

She would want him again.

Hell, she already wanted him again. Stepping into the club with him would only compound that desire into an irresistible urge.

Taking a deep breath, she swept her hair back over her shoulder, tilted her chin up and took the leap. She led him into the club, shaking her hands the whole time to try to ease the tension gradually building inside her as she waited for someone to notice him.

The patrons crowding the expansive dark room near the door were all human. Nothing for her to worry about.

She walked deeper, towards the long curved black bar to her right. Brightly lit bottles in a myriad of colours lined the wall behind it and spotlights above the bar changed from white to blue to purple to red, highlighting the patrons near it and those tending bar.

She nodded to one of the bartenders, a young female demon who wore human skin that would entice any man into flirting with her and leaving a good tip. She was pretty and innocent looking. Her wide dark eyes held a smile for every customer, male or female.

Taylor had met her in the field once or twice, and each time had ended up protecting her. Low-level demons like her were a tragedy waiting to happen. It was why Taylor had got her a job at the club where she would fall under the protection of the boss. No one bothered her now.

The woman slid her two shots of vodka. "On the house."

Taylor took them with a smile and turned to Einar.

She sensed the moment the first demon noticed him. It ran through the room like a current and every demon nearby turned their way, stopping in their tracks. The humans continued to dance, amongst other more sordid things, oblivious to what sort of creatures surrounded them.

Taylor knocked back the shot and held the other one out to Einar. He waved his hand in a silent refusal and she shrugged and then emptied the glass herself. Either alcohol was still a forbidden item for angels, one that would gain them instant punishment, or he didn't drink. Either way it was more for her and she needed it right now.

She ignored the demons that were looking their way. They were weak and of no concern to her, but she had to go deeper still into the club to find the boss, and she could sense stronger demons between her and her destination.

She tiptoed as she leaned back from the bar, looking over the heads of the throng of people to her left.

Dancers flickered in the strobe lights beyond those near her, writhing against each other, filling the room with the heavy scent of desire and the heat of their bodies.

She tried to take her eyes away, telling herself that she wasn't interested in the way they moved against each other, hands cupping and teasing, mouths fused together, bare flesh on show, but they wouldn't leave the dancers. It was erotic, sensual, and her temperature soared at just the sight of them.

They were oblivious to their onlookers. Or maybe they weren't. Maybe being watched was all part of their fun.

Her gaze lingered on one couple in particular, a male human and a female demon. They moved against each other, his naked chest brushing her barely concealed breasts as he skimmed his hands over her body. She turned in the his embrace, still dancing with him, grinding her backside against his groin. A smile curved both the man and the woman's lips when a second man joined in, palming the woman's breasts and kissing her as the first man kissed her shoulder and caressed her hips.

Taylor tore her gaze away, her heart fluttering and pulse racing. This sort of thing shouldn't be legal. The entire dance floor was bordering on becoming an orgy, alcohol and glamour fuelled, dangerous any way she looked at it.

Some demons weren't just here for a good night and a session of dirty dancing. There were those more sinister prowling the club, ones who were a deadly threat to the innocent humans.

She scanned the crowd and settled on a group of five male vampires leaning against the other end of the bar.

They were easy to spot for what they were.

Sharply dressed in black shirts and trousers, handsome and cool as they watched the crowd getting off on each other, they caught every woman's eye. Vampire charm was impenetrable, even for another demon. She couldn't see through their glamour. It was strong and it needed to be. It hid an ugly side best left for the kill rather than the hunt.

Taylor's attention stopped on one dark-haired vampire in particular when he leaned forwards and said something to one of the others.

She wasn't immune to their looks either. She had fallen for his handsomeness and toothy smile, and the promise of not being alone during the daylight hours. It had been good for a while. He had been more of a gentleman to her than most humans she had dated. He hadn't even bitten her until she had given him permission, and then he had chosen to sink his fangs into a place that ensured she had never forgotten him.

Her hand hovered over the spot on her inner thigh.

The vampire's pale gaze slid to her, as though she had called out to him by touching the marks.

His sensual dusky lips bowed into a smile and her heart fluttered, crimson touching her cheeks, until he said something to his four colleagues. They all looked her way, hungry intent in their pale eyes, a reminder of why things never would have worked between her and their leader.

Vampires were seducers by nature, addicted to the hunt and the kill. They were players. That wasn't the sort of man she wanted in her life.

"Do you know him?" The sound of Einar's bass voice, close to her ear, reassured her and soothed her tension.

Taylor nodded and then looked down when he touched her left arm, a jolt of surprise rocking her. The demons nearby stared. She didn't care. She looked over her shoulder and into his eyes.

His hard expression slowly changed to one of concern again and he slid his hand downwards. Her eyes briefly closed when his fingers tangled with hers and her heart beat harder. His touch was so comforting that she lost track of their surroundings.

It was only when she sensed danger that she snapped back to reality. She turned quickly, her right hand going for the blade strapped to her ribs beneath her jacket, and stopped with her hand on the hilt.

The vampire had come to see them.

CHAPTER 9

"Is he bothering you?" the vampire said, his smile masking the darkness Taylor could feel in him.

"I could ask the same thing." Einar pulled her closer to him.

The feathers of his wings tickled her arm when he brought it further back, so her hand was near his hip.

His sword.

He guided her hand to the hilt and she wrapped her fingers around it, following his silent instruction. It wouldn't come to a fight, but it was comforting to know that they were prepared for one nonetheless.

"Not at all. It's not like you to be jealous, Villandry." She shot the vampire a sweet smile.

Villandry cast his darkening gaze over her and then fixed it on Einar. Dark crimson ringed his irises, turning scarlet whenever the bar spotlights switched to red. His short neat hair turned as black as midnight and his pale skin looked even whiter when the lights switched to blue, as cold as his glare, but even that couldn't detract from his masculine beauty.

Women passing by stared at him and Taylor wondered if she had looked as hungry as them once, all those months ago, when she had fallen for Villandry's charm and beguiling smile. She shook away the memories of his slim toned physique and replaced them with images of how good Einar had looked naked, his broad muscled body bronzed and sexy. It was Einar who had the attention of her heart now, not Villandry. She wasn't going to fall for his glamour again.

His appearance was nothing but a lie. She had witnessed his true face before, the one he hadn't been able to hide in the heat of the moment when he had bitten her. He wasn't beautiful at all.

"What are you doing, Taylor, bringing one of their kind here? I take it you are not out to bring him to his knees?" Villandry's irises switched completely, burning scarlet, and his pupils narrowed and stretched, becoming cat-like.

She shook her head and her fingers flexed around Einar's sword. Villandry wouldn't see the action. Einar's tawny left wing obscured their hands. To Villandry, it would look as though Einar was holding her back.

Villandry sneered, flashing a hint of fang. "What business does he have here?"

"We have come for information." Einar's deep voice sent a shiver down her spine and her eyes widened slightly when he stepped into her, the full length of his body pressing against her back.

He placed his hand on her shoulder and then shifted it closer to her neck.

Closer to her blade.

Did he really think Villandry would be stupid enough to attack them in the club?

He had more class and sense than that. He was more likely to wait for them to finish their business and then track them when they left.

No matter how much they courted public attention, one thing would never change about vampires.

They liked to kill in private.

It was the reason they lived so long.

"I hardly thought you had come to partake in the party." Villandry ran his sharp gaze over them and settled it on her. "I am surprised the boss let you in with him. You know they are not to be trusted, Tay. Vile creatures. Take him away, Tay."

She hated that pet name of his. She had a perfectly good name, and she wasn't his to command, and he would do well to remember that.

She drew the shortest of her knives and had the tip of it against Villandry's throat before he could move. He didn't even tense. He calmly raised an eyebrow and looked down at her hand. The blade was small enough that most wouldn't notice it, barely the length of her thumb.

"We're just here for information. We'll be gone in a few minutes. Don't make this any more difficult than it already is, Villandry." She pressed the blade to his throat and the crimson bled from his eyes as he stared into hers. "And quit calling me Tay. It's been over a long time. Let it go."

"You wear my marks." Villandry's tone was as cold as ice as his gaze drilled into hers, black with the fury she could sense rising inside of him.

"It doesn't mean you own me. You can fool yourself if you like, but I'm not anyone's possession." Taylor pressed forward with the blade and then lowered her hand.

A thin dark line marked Villandry's throat.

She hadn't meant to cut him but perhaps it would help drive her point home without things turning violent. Nobody owned her. The marks on her thigh were just a scar now, regardless of how another vampire or Villandry might see them. They were just another memory.

"Taylor... I never thought you would turn out this way." Villandry touched his throat and then stared at the blood on his fingertips. He smeared it across them with his thumb, thoughtful and distant. She kept her guard up, unwilling to give him a chance to hurt her. His eyes met hers again and his expression hardened. He smiled and gave a short laugh, and then shook his head a fraction. "You think this story will have a happy ending? You are more of a fool than I had thought. It is one thing to work with such a vile creature, and another thing entirely to believe in anything it would say. Guard yourself, Taylor. The only thing you are heading for is a fall, and as you say, I do not own you, and therefore I will not be there this time to pick up the pieces."

Villandry disappeared.

She hated it when he did that.

She stepped forwards, out of the now cloying touch of Einar, and scanned the club for the vampire.

Einar placed his hand on her shoulder,

She rolled it, shirking his grip, and tiptoed, scouring the heaving room as she clenched her fists at her sides and gritted her teeth.

Bastard vampire.

Her heart slammed against her chest and stammered with the heavy beat of the music. Villandry had fired her up on purpose and then fled.

How dare he try to shake her faith in Einar?

She muttered a long string of obscenities that were blacker than Hell.

She sheathed her small knife against her ribs beneath her leather jacket, jamming it into the holster, rage pounding in her veins and demanding to be sated. Normally she would go out and find something to beat into oblivion when such a dark mood struck her. She couldn't do that with Einar in tow. Hell only knew what he thought of her now or how close he was to discovering secrets about her that she was desperate to keep hidden and fears she didn't want to face.

Villandry was right. She knew it deep in her heart. What she was doing with Einar was a mistake and it was going to go horribly wrong, and she couldn't see any way out of the impending disaster.

He was going to find out.

And then he was going to leave and break her heart.

And this time Villandry wouldn't be there.

She cursed again.

Einar touched her shoulder and she didn't shrug out of his grip this time. She let him touch her because she needed to feel his hands on her, feel him close to her, so she could fool herself into believing that Villandry was wrong. Einar wasn't going to hurt her.

"You slept with him?" There was darkness in his tone.

It carried his voice deep into her head and her heart over the music and she turned and raised her gaze to his. His eyes were black in the strobe light, no trace of gold in them now. Fury and a craving for violence trickled into her where his hand rested on her shoulder, the feeling creeping over her skin and warning her that making Einar jealous right now would be a very bad idea. She didn't know him well enough to judge what he might do, but the look in his eyes said that he would start by massacring the four vampires that Villandry had left behind.

"Once or twice, a long time ago." She placed her hand over his. "Don't tell me I have to use the 'let it go' speech on you too?"

The darkness in his eyes didn't shift.

She risked it and curled her fingers around his hand, holding it, and stepped closer to him. She didn't care if the demons were watching. Einar was too important to her for her to pretend that he meant nothing just so the demons wouldn't bother them. She wouldn't push him away like that, no matter what the consequences were. She couldn't.

"What's this all about, Taylor?" The high snappy tone of the woman's voice jolted her and she instantly released Einar's hand, her heart leaping into her throat.

She spun on her heel to face the woman.

The boss swept the short strands of her blonde hair from her dark eyes and locked gazes with her, looked so deep into them Taylor felt as though the boss was trying to probe her mind for the answer.

"Did you send a halfwit demon after us?" Taylor held her gaze, unflinching under the woman's scrutiny.

The boss's attention shifted to Einar.

And lingered.

Taylor frowned, a spear of jealousy lancing her chest, and was one step away from moving into the boss's line of sight when the woman looked back at her. Her expression turned harsh. Taylor had always thought the boss was pretty when she smiled. When she scowled, she was as ugly as sin and a flicker of her true appearance shifted over her skin, scaly and grotesque.

"Not after you. I was after those bastards." The boss waved a hand at a male bartender and before a minute had passed, he was handing her a tall dark drink.

Blood.

It wasn't just vampires that needed iron in their food.

The boss was a blood-drinker too and normally it came fresh from the vein. Taylor hoped that it hadn't tonight. She was sure that the boss had more sense than to have a human on tap when there was an angel in the room.

"No offence, Taylor, but what the fuck are you doing bringing one of his kind into my club?" the boss snapped, a flicker of fire in her eyes.

"Common purpose," Taylor blurted, feeling like a schoolkid all over again, afraid of her teacher's wrath. "We both want rid of these demons. It makes sense to work together."

"What you were doing a moment ago looked pretty damn far from just working together. I don't have to remind you how quickly this sort of shit goes bad." She swirled her glass of blood and lifted it to her nose, inhaled it as if savouring a fine wine, and then fixed a glare on Einar.

Taylor forced a smile. The boss certainly didn't have to remind her about the consequences of choosing Mr. Wrong, and Taylor suspected that she'd had her fair share of heartbreak too.

But it was different this time.

At least she hoped it was.

The last guy to break Taylor's heart had been one of Hell's guardians. The demon equivalent of an angel. That thought shook her. What if the good sort of angel broke her heart too? She wasn't sure which would hurt more—being jilted by one of her own kind, or by Einar.

"Just give me a break for a second and answer a few questions, and we'll be out of here." She placed her hands on her hips, gunning for confident and in control, and desperate to divert the course of their conversation.

She was tired of everyone telling her that she was heading for heartbreak when it was none of their business. She was certain that what she had with Einar wasn't going to backfire on her.

Well. Maybe seventy percent certain.

Fifty.

Whatever.

It didn't matter right now. She just needed answers from the boss about what had happened to the demon, any information that the woman had, and then she would be gone. When they were alone again, she was going to have a conversation with Einar, and at some point during it, she was going to find the courage to mention that one of her parents hadn't been human.

And hopefully he wouldn't send her to Heaven for questioning too.

The boss sipped her drink and pulled a thoughtful expression as her dark eyes narrowed on the liquid. Taylor started to lose what little patience she had left. People crowded them, pushing for room at the bar, and knocking against her. She was one shove away from snapping.

Einar moved so he was shielding her.

He placed one hand against the bar top, blocking access to her, and the boss formed the other wall. Damn, she appreciated the hell out of that, was thankful he could read her and had moved to help her without hesitation as her temperature started to lower again. She drew down a deep breath as she reined in her anger and blew it out, letting it all go. She had to keep a level head. Going nuclear on the patrons of the club for jostling her was as bad as bringing an angel into it.

"I thought those demons would come and see what had happened to their mate." The boss smiled and set her empty glass down on the dark bar top. Her look turned innocent. "I didn't think it would be you heading back that way."

"What happened the night before?" Einar's bass voice carried over the music.

The boss frowned at him, her pretty face twisting in a look of disgust that mixed with resignation as she sighed. Taylor hid her smile. The boss couldn't have made it more obvious that she didn't like giving information on demons to an angel if she had tried.

"I called in a favour and disposed of some garbage. Unfortunately, my favour was only good for one demon. Alexi is an extortionist. I couldn't afford the price he placed on the others." The boss gave Taylor a look that said 'you know what I mean'.

Taylor did.

She had worked with him once and had learned her lesson.

Alexi was a powerful demon, but he placed high prices on his services. His charge for all three demons had probably been the boss's soul.

The woman huffed. "So I sent the other demon after the remainder. You're not the only one who wants to see these bastards dead. They're bad for business."

"Bad for business? Why?" Taylor shot Einar a look that warned him to keep quiet this time.

This was her territory. It was better that she did the talking.

If Einar asked the questions, the boss would end up feeling as though she was under interrogation, and that would definitely get Taylor barred. It would also wreck their chance of getting the information she could feel the boss was close to giving them.

"Competition," the boss muttered but Taylor caught it.

Her gaze flickered to the dancers. "They're running a club?"

The boss glanced at the dance floor and then looked back at Taylor. She moved closer, and her gaze swept the room again before she spoke. Did she fear whoever they were after? It wasn't like the boss to be afraid. Demons worked for her because they knew she could handle anything in London, evil or good. There wasn't a demon out there that was a match for the boss when she was in a foul mood.

"It's a club, but that's not its purpose. That's just a front to get bodies through the door. They make out that they're like this place, somewhere humans can let go and do things with no regrets and no strings attached, but that isn't what's happening in there." The boss cast her gaze over the people nearby again and leaned in close to Taylor. Her voice lowered until Taylor barely heard her over the music. "It's Euphoria."

Taylor stepped back into the bar. She stared at the boss, her eyes wide as that word slowly sunk in.

"Euphoria?" Einar said and Taylor covered his mouth with her hand, and quickly looked around to make sure that no one else had heard him.

It couldn't be.

"You're sure?" She looked at the boss and released Einar's mouth.

The woman nodded. "I sent a couple of my boys in to check it out, ones who couldn't be traced to me."

"It would explain the body count." Taylor pressed her fist to her mouth.

This was bad.

Very bad.

Worse than she had imagined.

"We'll deal with it. Whereabouts is the club?" She wasn't sure they could deal with it, but she had to do something.

"Soho. I'll give you the address but they won't let you in." The boss jerked her chin towards Einar. "They'll spot him a mile away and shut down before you can get there. They keep watch."

Taylor frowned. There had to be a way into the club. She could go alone but something told her that Einar wouldn't agree to that, not if he knew what sort of hellhole the club would be.

Euphoria.

In all her years, she had never thought that a demon would dare start such a place in her city.

"You're sure they're dealing in it?" Because she wasn't, or maybe she just wanted this all to turn out to be a hoax, a joke on the boss's part.

The woman nodded.

There wasn't a hint of doubt in her eyes.

"Can you send a man there tonight? Someone who'll check out. He's got to be new here or the sort who'll frequent a lot of clubs. Someone the demons won't suspect." Taylor could see the mischief surfacing in the boss's eyes and shook her head, warning her not to even think about picking that damned bastard.

The woman smiled and glanced at Einar. "I know just the man. No one would suspect him."

Taylor groaned at that, hoping she was wrong but aware that the way her luck was going, the man was going to be tall, dark and undead. It was just like the boss to choose the one man who could jeopardise whatever she had with Einar. She probably thought it was funny.

Taylor didn't.

"Just send him in to confirm it and then we'll send him back to lure the ringleaders out. We'll deal with them tonight," she bit out, her mood darkening at the thought of what was going to happen.

Maybe there was a way she could minimise the fallout from the boss's meddling?

Maybe snowballs really wouldn't melt in Hell.

The boss winked and disappeared into the crowd. Taylor looked up at Einar, expecting his eyes to be on her.

"A club like this?" He glanced at her and then looked over her head again.

"No. This is civilised." Taylor looked around, not missing that the demons nearby were still watching them. "We'll talk about it en route."

"She is going to get that vampire, isn't she?" The darkness in his voice as he said that gave his words more bite than the vampire in question.

There was no fooling Einar. Which meant, there was also no point in lying to him.

She nodded.

She had been wondering how she was going to break it to him. At least one thing was out in the open. Now she just had to say the other. She couldn't do it here. She didn't want an audience.

There was one thing she could say though.

"I feel nothing for Villandry," she said and his gaze flickered to her and then he looked beyond her again.

"Good." That word was harsh, barked from between clenched teeth.

His expression softened as she stared up at him and then shifted, feelings crossing it she couldn't decipher.

His eyes darkened.

What was he looking at?

Was it the other vampires?

When she turned and followed his gaze, her heart skipped a beat.

He was watching the dancers.

She had almost forgotten they were there. Her eyes fixed on the couples nearest the edge of the dance floor and desire beat through her veins in time with the music, a pounding hard rhythm that had her shifting on the spot and drove thoughts of dancing like that with Einar through her mind.

She pictured them on the dance floor, her fingers wandering across his broad bare chest, teasing his pebbled nipples, fingernails raking over his stomach muscles and leaving red marks in their wake. She imagined the feel of his body against hers, as hot and hard as it had been last night, brushing her as he moved with her, his hands coursing over her arms and sides, caressing her hips and breasts.

She wanted to feel that and she wanted to do those things, in public, with him. The thought of it fired her up, sending tingles of desire rippling through her body.

She turned again and stared into Einar's dark eyes. His wide pupils engulfed his irises. She could sense his restraint as it mirrored hers, and his battle against his desire. He wanted it too.

His gaze fell and met hers. Her heart beat harder, thumping against her chest, driven by anticipation.

He reached out and swept his fingers along her jaw and then down her neck, his touch light and teasing. She shivered when he brushed them over her throat, clearing her long black hair from it, and frowned. She knew what he was looking for but he wouldn't find them there. She would never have let Villandry mark her in such a prominent place.

Einar's thumb caressed the line of her jaw and then her cheek. Her eyelids slipped to half-mast when he lightly ran the pad of it over her lower lip and then she looked up at him through her lashes. Her lips parted and she breathed hard, wrestling for restraint that seemed impossible to obtain.

She wanted him. Needed him. Ached for him. It pounded in her body, thrummed in her veins, compelling her to satisfy her deep hunger to kiss and touch him. The look in his eyes, the fascination as he watched his thumb tease her lip, said he felt the same.

It was wrong of them but she didn't care. She needed him.

Her kind can think what they wanted about her.

Because she could only think about him.

CHAPTER 10

"What is Euphoria?" Einar looked out over the dark city, his gaze scanning the adjacent rooftops of the elegant red brick and sandstone buildings and then the street below.

Taylor stood beside him, her arms wrapped tightly around herself, holding her leather jacket closed.

The temperature had dropped, and not just in the city.

It had fallen cold between them too.

He didn't mean for it to be that way, but he couldn't help it. Whenever he thought about the fact Taylor had slept with that vampire, the same vampire they had been forced to travel across the city with, he bristled and wanted to kill something.

It wasn't her fault.

He couldn't blame her for something that had happened before they had even met.

His foul mood was due to the vampire.

Villandry had passed the entire taxi journey to Soho staring at Taylor, making lewd allusions to their past trysts, and pretending that he owned her.

It was enough to make Einar want to kill him. He didn't even care that it would have ruined their hunt for the demons and their chance to capture them. He would have killed him the moment they were in private, away from mortal eyes, if it hadn't been for Taylor.

While Villandry had paid constant attention to her, her attention had been firmly locked on him instead of the vampire. She had even gone as far as openly touching his hand at one point, and he had taken comfort from it, together with the sliver of control he had needed to stop him from twisting the damned vampire's head off.

As if she knew his thoughts, her hand brushed his, bringing him back to the rooftop and her. She stroked the backs of her fingers across his and he closed his eyes and tangled their hands together. He breathed deep, wanting to let his anger go so things between them would be fine again, but it was difficult.

"He means nothing to me."

Those words were sweet reassurance. Honey to his heart.

He shifted his gaze to meet hers. She smiled, stunning in the low light, her dark hair tied back into a neat ponytail now and exposing the full extent of her beauty.

"Although... I don't mind seeing you jealous." Her smile grew a little wicked and teasing.

Jealous wasn't a strong enough word for how he felt.

There should be another word for the possessive, murderous rage inside him. Something stronger.

"Tell me," he said and her eyes widened, her heartbeat picking up a note of fear.

Einar smiled to reassure her that he wasn't asking her to confess her feelings or anything of that sort. He wasn't going to push her because he knew how difficult this was for her. It was difficult for both of them. Impossible. Yet he still wanted to give it his best shot and convince her that it would work out between them and that there was no reason for her to flip between wanting him and wanting to leave.

No matter what she thought, he wasn't going to hurt her.

"Euphoria." That single word brought relief to her eyes.

She gazed into the distance, the chill breeze tousling strands of her ponytail, and sighed.

She was beautiful with London as her backdrop, the dark city pricked with lights that shone like stars.

76

"It used to be common." She brushed her hair back, tucking the rogue threads behind her ears with her free hand. "Cloud Nine doesn't supply drugs or anything other than alcohol and a place to free your inhibitions. Dealing in Euphoria is different to that. Humans think they're getting drug-laced cocktails to help them unwind. What they're getting is far worse."

She faced him, her blue eyes meeting his, sharp and serious.

"It's demon toxin."

Shock rippled through him. "But that would kill—"

He saw in her eyes that she was telling the truth. Her reaction and that of the boss back at the club told him that there were demons who were against such a thing, and it had surprised him to hear it. He was beginning to realise that not all demons were out to harm humans, that what he had been taught as an angel was wrong. Or at least it was wrong in this era.

There were demons who wanted to protect the mortals as fiercely as the angels did.

Was it Taylor's part-human blood that drove her to defend her city against those who sought to hurt it? Or was it her demon blood?

"The theory goes that you give them only a drop, so they become compliant and dazed. It's mixed with something else to make them a slave to the demon whose toxin they've imbibed." Taylor shivered and released his hand. She wrapped her arms around herself again and stared into the night. "Euphoria isn't about the thrill it gives the humans and the demons. It's purely about the demons. The excitement of controlling someone like a slave, of making them do things, of being able to do as they please with a mortal. Drink from them, screw them, beat them. Anything goes."

"Including killing them?" The thought that it might had that uncontrollable rage boiling back to life in his veins and he clenched his fists and glared at the city, a hunger to hunt down every wretch who used Euphoria on a human beating inside him.

"Death doesn't normally come into it. The amount of toxin should be small enough that it can't kill, so the human involved doesn't become sick, but there's always the risk of something going wrong. A trip on Euphoria should always end with the demon administering an antidote. The human wakes up feeling fine and on top of the world, unaware of the things they

did. I've seen it in other cities, and every demon knows the rules of play."
Taylor frowned, a flicker of concern crossing her delicate features as she
shook her head. "This isn't Euphoria as most demons know it. Something
else is happening at that club, and we need to find out what it is."

Her gaze shifted to him and gone was the worry. There was only
confidence and determination. It shone in her blue eyes, luring him back
under her spell, conjuring images of her fighting that stirred a different
feeling in his blood—desire.

"We will put an end to this, Taylor," he growled and settled his hand on
the sword sheathed at his waist.

They would discover what was happening and he would deal with the
demons responsible.

He placed his free hand on her slender shoulder, her leather jacket cold
beneath his fingers. She started to smile and then frowned again. Her eyes
searched his, flicking between them, and her lips parted, and he sensed the
struggle within her.

"Einar." She hesitated and dropped her gaze to his feet before slowly
working it back up his body. "I... I'm... I have to tell you something... and,
well, here goes nothing... I'm—"

He tensed at the same time as she did. "I felt that too."

Something had shot through him, a sense that danger was approaching,
like ice chasing down his spine beneath his armour. Taylor's head snapped
around and she gasped. He followed the direction of her gaze and saw why.

Villandry was leaping from roof to roof across the city, heading towards
them, and he wasn't alone. Two black demons were in pursuit, barely
visible in the night sky, their scaly dark wings beating the air.

They were closing in on the vampire. And they were closing in fast.

"It's them," she said, voicing his thoughts for him.

Einar grabbed her, leaped onto the low wall surrounding the flat roof
and kicked off. He beat his wings hard, shooting towards Villandry. As
little as he liked the vampire, he couldn't let the demons kill him. The male
had helped him after all, luring his prey out into the open for him.

The shadowy demons swooped on the vampire as he hit a long roof
with a glass skylight running along the centre of it. Villandry ducked and

strafed left, dodging the first demon, and hit the deck when the second lashed out at him. He rolled to his feet and kept sprinting towards the other end of the roof.

Einar looked there. It was a dead end, unless the vampire intended to leap the more than one hundred foot gap between the building he was on and the next one. Einar twisted and swept lower, beat his wings harder as he raced to reach Villandry before it was too late.

The dark-haired vampire skidded to a halt near the end of the roof, the pitched glass windows casting golden light over his left side, warming his pale skin and the black suit he wore. He breathed hard, staring across the distance to the next building.

He wouldn't make it.

Could he teleport that far? The vampire had disappeared in Cloud Nine, revealing a power that had surprised Einar. He had never heard of vampires teleporting before and had immediately filed it with Heaven for their records of the species.

Villandry's shoulders relaxed, he straightened to his full height and slowly pivoted on his heel to face the two demons. Madness. The vampire possessed no weapons. He was no match for the demons when they were armed with talons on both their hands and their feet.

It didn't stop the male.

He launched at the demons, targeting the smaller of the two first, and grunted as they collided hard, the sound loud in the still air. He was swift as he blocked every blow the demons aimed at him, each slash of their tails and snap of their fangs, and managed to land a few of his own, clawing at the creatures and leaving long grooves in their black skin.

Einar increased his speed, clinging to Taylor so he wouldn't drop her, because there was no way Villandry could hold them off for long, let alone defeat them without a weapon.

She drew her short blade and twisted out of his arms the moment they were above the roof, landed on her feet in a crouch and sprinted towards the vampire.

"Villandry," she hollered as she reached down to her side.

The vampire turned and caught the blade she tossed to him, nodding as he gripped it and spun to face his opponents again.

The demons swiped at him, claws long and slashing, but Villandry dodged or blocked every attempt, and lashed out with the short blade gripped fiercely in his hand. The smaller demon hissed as it made contact and recoiled, beating its shadowy wings to gain some space.

Another blessed blade?

Taylor came up beside the vampire, her sword a bright silver arc in the darkness as she kept the smaller demon on the back foot, forcing him further away from his companion.

Einar drew his own sword, pinned his wings back and dropped hard, landing before the second demon. He pressed his left boot into the tar roof and lunged, swiping his blade up in a fast arc. The demon hissed and leaned backwards, and wind battered Einar as it beat its wings.

When the demon rallied and attacked, Einar kicked backwards, using his wings to propel him and luring the demon with him, leaving Taylor and Villandry to deal with the other.

The warm glow from the skylight chased over the demon, revealing it to him. It was almost human in form, but where a nose should have been there was nothing but two holes flat against its scaly skin. A wide mouth cut across the oval of its face, almost reaching from ear to ear, and a pair of large almond-shaped vivid yellow eyes focused on him with deadly intent.

The demon snarled, exposing pointed teeth that were almost as black as its skin, and lunged at him. Einar dodged its hand talons. Fighting in mid-air was never easy. In fact, he hated it. Battles were best fought on the ground, where he could easily avoid his enemy's attacks and defeat him.

It was difficult to keep his focus on his opponent as the sound of fighting rang up from below, a masculine grunt mingling with the softer sounds of Taylor as she battled the smaller demon.

He beat his wings to place some more distance between him and his own demon. It studied him as it flew around, prowling the night sky, its huge dragon-like wings beating the chilly air.

It made another sharp lunge, swiping at him with the claws on its feet. Einar avoided the blow and swept left, keeping the distance between them steady as he assessed the demon. It moved with him, keeping the gap between them steady, and then attacked again, twice in a row, little jabs with its hands that carried an air of indifference, as though it was merely testing him.

They were both looking for an opening.

The demon shifted backwards in the sky and its thin pupils darted to the fight happening below them. Einar beat his wings and shot towards the demon. He brought his sword back, close to his side, and then thrust the blade forwards as he reached the demon. The demon turned in the air, avoiding the attack but not completely. The tip of Einar's sword caught its left wing, slicing through the black membrane, and the demon cried out.

The screech pierced Einar's ears and he flinched as they rang.

He attacked again, feinting right and then going left to sweep around behind the demon. He kicked the creature in the back, sending it tumbling forwards in the air, and swept down towards it as it struggled to right itself. The demon evaded the blow he aimed at its back, twisted in the air as it dropped beyond his reach and stretched its talons out and slashed at him.

Einar dodged right with a hard beat of his wings, narrowly missing the demon's claws. He wasn't immune to the toxin that demons produced. If it caught him, he would suffer worse than a human. His angel blood saw to that.

The other demon screeched and someone yelled at the same time.

His heart froze in his chest.

His eyes leaped down to the roof below him.

CHAPTER 11

Relief beat through Einar as he saw Taylor was fine. She knelt on the roof, supporting Villandry, fear written on every beautiful line of her face as she tried to rouse the vampire. The demon he had been fighting dived towards them. Einar clutched his sword and swooped, his focus locked on the wretch.

He had to stop it from attacking Taylor.

He had to protect her.

She picked up her sword from the roof beside her, a grim look of determination on her face as she rose onto her feet and stared the demon down.

It grinned.

Einar threw his hand out and three narrow shafts of white light shot towards the demon. It snarled and dodged the first two but the third impaled its right thigh and its snarl became a shriek as it ground to a halt and turned on him.

He didn't hesitate. He saw his chance and took it.

Raising his hand towards the sky, he used all the strength he could spare to call on Heaven.

A bright beam shot down, capturing two thirds of the demon.

His aim was off.

He moved his hand to one side to shift the beam and incarcerate the rest of the demon to stop it from escaping.

White-hot pain exploded in his side.

Einar swallowed and looked down, staring in disbelief at the three black spikes sticking out of his skin above his right hip.

"Die," the demon behind him hissed as it twisted its hand and yanked its talons out of Einar's side.

He threw his head back and bellowed as an inferno spread outwards from his side, swiftly engulfing him and sending his vision wobbling. The white beam flickered, stuttering as his focus shattered. The demon encased in it growled and began to break free, clawing towards the edge of the light.

No.

Einar wouldn't allow it. He scoured the roof for Taylor, blinking as he fought the effect of the demon toxin as it swiftly entered his blood. Sweat broke out across his brow and his body, and he shivered as the fiery fever raced through him.

He blinked again, widened his eyes and growled as he struggled to regain his focus. Another shiver wracked him and his teeth chattered as he stretched his hand out and put all of his remaining strength into holding the second demon and protecting Taylor.

She wavered in and out of focus as she looked up at him, her dark eyebrows furrowing and blue eyes shimmering with tears as she shook her head. Her lips moved but he couldn't hear her words. His vision distorted, darkness encroaching at the edges of it.

He had to hold on and finish the demon.

He couldn't fail her.

She moved, racing towards the beam of light. The demon struggled but didn't stand a chance. She brought her sword up in a swift arc and cut off its head.

Einar silently thanked her for ending his need to contain the demon and pressed his hand to his side. Blood pumped through his fingers, hot but swiftly chilling as it cascaded down his hip. He swallowed and turned, his head throbbing and dark waves washing over him, and looked for the other demon.

It was gone.

His sword slipped from his hand and fell into the street far below.

Einar tipped back, lost his fight to remain conscious, and followed it.

He didn't feel the impact, or hear Taylor screaming his name. He felt nothing in the endless black, surrounded by warmth and peace.

He knew nothing.

And then a voice.

It called to him.

He heard it not in his ears but in his heart.

And he responded.

He sucked air into his bruised lungs.

Obeyed that whispered demand not to leave her.

Taylor.

He lurched off the ground.

Only it wasn't the broken asphalt of the road.

Strong hands pinned his shoulders and he fought the person seeking to restrain him. He had to move. He had to get up and move. Taylor was calling him. She was hurting and afraid. He needed to go to her.

Einar pushed the person away. There was a crash and they cursed in Taylor's sweet voice.

Before he could move, the hands were back against him. A swirl of voices rang out in the room, incomprehensible, foreign. It was a language that he didn't understand but one that provoked a response in him.

Strength surged through him and he knocked the person aside, driven by the fury of hearing demonic words uttered in his presence.

Demons.

He would kill them if they had hurt Taylor.

"Keep still, you big oaf!" Taylor's sweet voice again. "Can't you give him something to knock him out?"

"I am a little busy trying to stem the bleeding!" The vampire.

Hands pressed on his shoulders again but this time Einar remained still. He focused, bringing his senses back into order, and mentally checked himself over. His side burned as though someone had poured acid in the wound and he was weak, muscles like water beneath his skin as his strength drained from him again.

Demon toxin.

He remembered that now.

He had tried to protect Taylor and the demon had seized the opportunity to kill him.

Only he wasn't dead.

He opened his eyes but the world remained black. Pain shot through his body when he moved, pulsing in strong waves that made him sick. He swallowed it down and tried to sit up.

"Keep still," Taylor whispered and stroked his cheek.

Einar collapsed back, willing to do as she had said because he didn't have the strength to move anyway.

"Dark." He pushed the word out and swallowed again, this time trying to wet his throat so he could speak.

"Stay there a little longer." Taylor's fingers grazed his jaw, her touch soft and tender, soothing the pain inside him. "You can come back soon. You were supposed to stay asleep."

Was he? What had she done to him? Was this one of her powers, or the vampire's?

He had been out cold and not because of the fall or the toxin. It had been something else. She had sent him somewhere that had felt like death only devoid of any other souls.

"Heard you," he muttered and fought to remain conscious when she pressed her hand to his forehead.

"I'm sorry. I didn't mean to disturb you." She leaned in, until he could smell her warm fragrance and feel her breath on his face.

Her damp cheek touched his and she stayed there, lingering with it pressed gently against his.

Was she crying for his sake?

He didn't want to make her cry. He was strong enough to survive demon toxin.

For her.

"Sleep a while. Pleasant dreams, Romeo." She brushed her lips across his cheek and the darkness swept over him again.

Was that where she had sent him? Deep into some dream world to take him away from reality and the pain?

He tried to hold on, wanted to stay with her, but the pull was too strong and he slipped into the endless black.

It was different this time.

The darkness faded to reveal a beautiful green valley stretched before him, hills rolling down towards a sparkling river and the clumps of trees that lined it. Bright sunlight beat on him from a cerulean sky that stretched on forever into the distance, beyond hazy mountains. He sighed and took it all in, studying the details that had gone into creating such a peaceful place. Sheep roamed the hill down from him and a red kite flew overhead, calling to another across the valley bottom.

Einar wasn't sure how long he was there. Time lost meaning and he didn't feel the minutes pass as he watched life happening. He sat on the grass, letting the scenery wash over him, studying every little detail, from the leaves on the trees to the way the river caught the light as it snaked across the valley.

With a long sigh, he lay back and stretched out, the blades of grass tickling his arms and sides as he stared up at the sky.

The red kite flew overhead. Majestic and beautiful. Wings still as it cut through the warm air. Calling again. He stretched his hand up to it, as though he could touch it from so far away, and smiled.

It was so tranquil.

The sun warmed his skin, the sounds of the world drifted around him, and he found himself closing his eyes to savour the feel of this place that Taylor had created for him.

When he opened them again, a grotty white room had replaced the beautiful valley.

"You're awake." Taylor leaned over him. Her dark eyebrows furrowed as she brushed her fingers over his brow. "How are you feeling?"

He mentally checked himself over again and his eyebrows lifted when he felt no pain.

"Fine." Einar frowned and looked down the length of his body.

His dark brown breastplate was gone but the rest of his armour remained. His wings were gone too. They must have disappeared when he had lost consciousness, so he would look human to anyone who found him.

He focused to keep them away and stared at his waist. White bandages covered it, stained crimson on his right side.

Taylor lightly touched his stomach and her voice shook. "We can't heal you like angels can. Villandry removed the poison and stitched the wounds. I bandaged you."

"And sent me to somewhere else," he murmured, sure he would never forget the beautiful place she had chosen for him.

She refused to look at him, kept her blue eyes fixed on her hand where it rested on his stomach.

He placed his hand over hers and she stared at them.

She was trembling.

Why?

"Do you hate me?" Tears slipped down onto her cheeks and she closed her eyes.

His heart ached at the sight of them and the feel of her in so much pain.

"Never, Taylor. Why would you think such a thing?" He squeezed her hand so she would look at him.

The ache in his chest worsened when she didn't do as he wanted. She kept her eyes closed, screwing them shut so tightly that she was frowning, as though she couldn't bring herself to face him.

As though she couldn't bring herself to look at him for some reason.

"You know what I am now." She bit her lip when a sob pushed free.

Einar pulled her to him.

She stumbled and landed heavily on him, knocking his wounds and sending pain sparking along every nerve. He didn't care.

He wrapped her in his arms and held her head to his bare chest. She cried then, sobbing against him in a way that broke his heart as he stroked her black hair, running his fingers through her long ponytail in an attempt to soothe her. He dropped his hand to her back, rubbed it through her black camisole and just held her, sure that it would give her the comfort she needed.

She suddenly pulled back, her lashes wet with the tears that streaked her cheeks, and looked at him, a myriad of feelings dancing in her eyes as they searched his. Fear broke to the surface, together with pain that beat inside him too, because he knew what had caused her tears, and it was his fault for not telling her sooner.

He lifted his hand and gently cupped her cheek.

"Taylor." He brushed her tears away with his thumb and she dropped her gaze to his chest. He pressed his fingers under her jaw and tilted her head back so she would look at him, because she needed to see he was telling her the truth. "I have always known."

Her deep blue eyes widened and she blinked.

"I knew, and maybe it mattered to me at first, but not now. I do not care that it is forbidden, and I was not lying when I told you that I do not think it is wrong." He stroked her cheek, his eyebrows furrowing as he smoothed her tears away and absorbed the feel of her beneath his fingers, how soft and warm she was, and how she filled his heart with light. "Nothing that makes me feel this way could ever be wrong."

Her smile started out shaky but then it curved her lips, she pressed her hands to his pectorals and leaned over him. He closed his eyes as his lips met hers and wrapped her in his arms again, keeping the kiss light.

He wanted to show her that it didn't matter that she was a demon, not to him.

She was his beautiful Taylor.

And he was falling in love with her.

CHAPTER 12

Taylor helped Einar off the hospital bed in the small basement medical centre, caving and giving in to him. She had tried keeping him in bed, but he was a terrible patient, kept demanding she let him up and saying he had work to do. When that failed, he tried to bribe her with kisses.

Those almost worked.

Scratch that.

They had worked.

Her lips still tingled from their last round of kissing, the earthy spicy taste of him lingering on her tongue. She wanted to kiss him again, but getting fired up wasn't going to do her or him any favours. He needed to recover from the hell he had gone through.

Hell that still tore at her heart, had her feeling weak at times, her limbs trembling as she recalled watching him plummet from the sky and everything that had happened afterwards.

His tawny wings grew out of his back and unfurled, and he leaned his ass against the edge of the gurney as he stretched them and inspected them, preening them.

She kept hold of his arm, afraid that it was too soon to move him and that he would hurt himself. She had never realised that demon toxin was certain death to angels. When Villandry had told her that, her heart had beat so hard she had felt as though it was going to stop.

It had taken all of her power to give Einar peace and comfort whilst Villandry had done his best to filter his blood and remove the toxin. She was actually glad now that the boss had chosen him as their bait. It had been too late to call the doctor in and the nurse had been useless.

Villandry's knowledge of how blood worked and how to cleanse it of poison quickly and effectively had been the only thing that had saved Einar.

She hadn't been able to do anything for him.

Except send him to sleep.

And even then he had awoken.

How?

Einar had said that he had heard her. She hadn't spoken his name or said a word to him the whole time that Villandry had been working on the wound. Had he heard her speaking to Villandry, or had he heard something else?

He reached out and stroked his fingers down her cheek, drawing her back to him.

"You are scared," he whispered.

"I almost lost you." She lifted her eyes to meet his rich brown ones, lost herself in them as the golden flecks in them barely shifted.

He smiled but she could see the strain in it. Standing was causing him pain. She wanted to make him rest again, but knew in her heart he wouldn't listen to her now that he was back on his feet. He would probably kiss her again to silence her.

Maybe it would be worth the hassle just so she could have that kiss.

She needed one right now.

She needed answers too though.

"You said that you heard me." Taylor stopped herself.

What she wanted to ask him sounded ridiculous even to her and she was sure he would laugh at her for thinking such nonsense.

What if it were true though? What if he had heard her and it hadn't been her voice that had spoken to him?

She jumped when his hand came to rest heavily on her chest, fingers splaying out and the heel of his palm between her breasts. She stared down at it, wishing they were flesh to flesh, not hindered by her black camisole.

She needed to feel his hands on her, warm and caressing, making her feel alive.

"You called me back," he whispered and took her hand and placed it on his bare chest, right over his heart. He held it there, pressing against his warm flesh, and she stared at it a moment and then into his eyes. "I heard you, Taylor. Not in my ears, but here in my heart. Yours to mine."

A shiver danced through her.

When he had been lying on the bed, bleeding, dying, she hadn't been able to find her voice to speak to him and tell him to come back to her. She had done so in silence, with all of her heart, confessing everything to him.

She needed him.

He couldn't die, because she couldn't live without him.

It didn't matter that it was forbidden.

She was in love with him.

Taylor closed her eyes when he leaned forwards and captured her lips. His kiss was soft and gentle, stirring her feelings and warming her through as it brought tears to her eyes and everything came rushing back.

She had almost lost him. She didn't want that to happen, not for any reason. She needed him too much.

He hissed and sucked in a sharp breath.

She broke away from his lips, ignored his muttered protest as she took hold of his shoulders and moved him back.

He pressed his hand to his side and her eyes widened when the red stain there grew, seeping outwards across the bandages. She didn't want to look at them, wanted to forget everything that had happened, but she couldn't convince her eyes to move away.

"Maybe I should take care of these first." Einar's fingers flexed against his side.

Taylor stepped back when light filtered out from between his fingers. Was he healing himself?

"I didn't know you could do that," she said.

He smiled but it was a thin line, his lips compressed and a frown of concentration etched on his handsome face. It looked more like a grimace to Taylor.

"I cannot rid myself of toxin." He closed his eyes and the light grew brighter as he sagged harder against the bed.

Taylor shielded her eyes as the light filled the room.

He drew a long deep breath, sounding strained as he said, "I can heal wounds... though... it takes great effort to do so on myself."

His hand fell away from his side and he leaned back against the bed on his elbows, his stomach muscles rippling with each deep breath he took. His eyes closed and his jaw tensed.

Had he managed to heal himself?

He seemed weaker to her now.

Normally he was strong on her senses and they warned her of his power, but now he barely registered. He hadn't felt so weak after he had healed her.

Was it the cycle of power that made it difficult to heal himself?

She couldn't give herself pleasant dreams. Her power resisted itself. Perhaps it was the same for Einar.

She reached out and swept her fingers over the bandage. His stomach tensed, muscles flexing as she stroked around the bloodstains, her eyes on them, monitoring them so she could reassure herself that he was healed now.

His eyes slowly opened and she raised hers to meet them. His breathing steadied but grew heavier as he stared deep into her eyes, his pupils dilating to devour the earthy brown of his irises and the golden flecks that swirled in them.

Taylor arched an eyebrow.

She didn't think he was up for the sort of activity she could feel as a need running through him and see in his eyes, but she didn't take her hand away. She grazed her fingers over his bare stomach, following the line of the bandage, and found the point where she had pinned it in place.

His gaze held hers as she unpinned the white fabric and he sat up as she unravelled it. Each time she leaned towards him to reach around his back, he kissed her shoulder or her cheek, teased and tortured her with the soft warm feel of his lips and a silent promise she knew he could come good on. When he was at full strength anyway.

The air in the room thickened as she removed the bandages, weathering his assault, until she was breathing as hard as he was, battling her rising desire.

Now wasn't the time for such things and it certainly wasn't the place.

While Einar was the only patient in this room of the medical centre, Villandry was still in the other room with the day nurse.

Taylor's eyes widened when the last length of bandage fell away, revealing Einar's stomach. She ran her fingers over the perfect skin on his right side.

Not even a scar remained.

Her gaze snapped to his when he took hold of her hand, bringing it away from his stomach and up to his lips.

He kissed her fingers and then opened her palm and pressed a kiss there. Her lips parted when he kissed her wrist and then along her forearm, bringing her towards him at the same time.

"Einar," she murmured and her cheeks coloured when he smiled wickedly.

"You only seem to say my name at times like this." He pressed another kiss to the soft skin of her forearm and then the inside of her elbow.

She didn't know what he was talking about. She was sure that she had said it at other times too. She had screamed it at the top of her lungs when he had fallen out of the sky.

Taylor closed her eyes against the memory. She didn't want to remember it or how scared she had been.

It had felt as though her whole world had been falling apart.

"What is wrong?" Einar touched her cheek and she leaned into his hand, unable to stop herself and desperately needing the comfort of his touch to ease her pain and convince her that he was alive, fine now.

She wasn't going to lose him.

She turned her face and kissed his palm, breathed him in and savoured the smell of him. He was here now. Alive. Unharmed. A tear slid down her cheek.

"Taylor," Einar breathed and pulled her into his arms, gathering her close. She closed her eyes when his wings wrapped around her too, covering her completely, and he pressed a kiss to her forehead. "I am sorry I scared you."

She drew back, settled her palms against his bare chest, and looked up into his eyes.

There was such a beautifully honest and tender look in them. She believed everything he had told her earlier. She believed that he didn't care that she was part-demon and that this was a sin for both of them.

She believed that beating inside him were feelings that echoed hers.

She snaked her arms around his neck and captured his lips, fusing her mouth with his and sliding her tongue along the seam of his. He opened for her and she sighed as his tongue teased the sensitive flesh on the inside of her lips. It tickled, waves of shivers rolling through her in response, and she closed her eyes, tilted her head to one side, and kissed him harder, tangling her tongue with his and savouring the feel of him against her.

He was flesh and blood, no longer in pain or close to dying. He was back with her, where he belonged, and she could feel him growing stronger again.

He kissed along her jaw, open mouthed and rough, nipping occasionally. Each bite with his blunt teeth shot her temperature up another degree, and she was burning for him by the time he reached her throat.

He devoured it with hungry kisses and bites, bathed it with his tongue and sucked on it, sparking pain through her chased by pleasure. It built inside her, pushing her doubts and fears to the back of her mind where they belonged, filling her head with thoughts of them together, naked and writhing. She wanted to pull him off the bed and dance flesh-to-flesh with him as the people had at the club. She wanted to shed her inhibitions and embrace her desire for Einar.

He groaned against her shoulder and buried his face in her neck, sucking her skin and kissing her roughly. His fingers dug into her sides, his grip on her so strong that it thrilled her. She leaned into his hungry mouth and tilted her head to one side, shivers cascading along her arms and down her back and chest with each bite and lick. Her nipples tightened, taut against her black bra and top, aching for his attention as need bloomed in her.

A noise in the other room made her freeze. She tensed in his arms, her heart pounding.

He didn't stop, not even when she tried to push him off her.

"Do not worry," he whispered and kissed her throat below her ear.

One hand left her side and he waved it towards the door. Locks clicked into place. It would stop Villandry from entering easily but it wouldn't stop him from sensing what was happening in the room.

Einar's persuasive kisses chased her worries away until they were slipping out of her head again and she could only focus on the delicious feel of him.

"Tell me what you were thinking earlier... back at the club," he husked in her ear and she trembled, her eyes closing as she remembered how she had felt when watching the dancers and imagining doing the same with Einar. He kissed her earlobe and then licked it. His warm breath teased her ear. "When you saw those people dancing..."

The vision of them cranked up the heat until she was burning hotter than Hell for Einar.

She grabbed him around the neck and kissed him, pouring her passion into it until she could barely breathe, until it was wild and choppy, a fierce meeting of lips that had an inferno igniting inside her. It still wasn't enough. She wanted him so much that it blazed through her, a wildfire that threatened to consume her completely if she didn't get it under control.

"I was thinking that I wanted to do that..." she whispered into his mouth and swept her tongue over his lower lip. He groaned and tried to kiss her but she drew back and looked deep into his beautiful golden eyes. "I wanted to do that with you."

"Taylor," he uttered and grabbed her.

She gasped when he twisted and slammed into the wall with her, his hands firmly gripping her thighs and his body wedged between them. He ground against her. She moaned and ran her hands over his strong arms, fingertips traversing his tensed muscles, a shiver running through her at the feel of the power he commanded. He went to work on her throat again, covering it with rough kisses that stoked the fire inside her as she leaned her head back, giving him access to her.

She skimmed her fingers over his broad shoulders, up his corded neck, and buried them in the tawny lengths of his ponytail. He groaned and kissed her ear, her jaw, the corner of her mouth. She tilted her head and captured his lips, swallowing another moan, and bucked against him.

She wanted to feel him. Skin on skin.

She pushed against his shoulders, forcing him back. His eyes darkened, nostrils flaring and eyebrows knitting hard as she fought to remove her top.

He set her down and made fast work of her clothes, tossing each item onto the bed beside them. Her fingers shook with urgent need as she tackled his armour, stripping off his vambraces and the armour around his hips, and fighting his damned loincloth.

She fell back against the wall when he bent down and tugged her jeans with him, and almost fell over when he tried to pull them off over her boots.

He said something in a language she didn't understand.

It sounded dark and menacing, and a lot like swearing.

The ground shook.

Her eyes widened.

Angels clearly shouldn't cuss.

He chased that thought away too when he glared at her jeans tangled in her boots and both items of clothing disappeared, leaving her bare. That was cheating. She couldn't do that with his clothes.

She didn't have to. His loincloth, greaves and boots disappeared in a flash. She was about to commend him on what was turning out to be a rather handy ability when he took hold of her left ankle, slung her leg over his shoulder so it rested beside his wing, and raised her.

Taylor gasped at the first stroke of his tongue against her most sensitive area.

He groaned and slipped his fingers into her warm folds, parting them and tasting her again. She shivered and leaned back into the wall for support as he licked her, teasing her pert arousal with a talented tongue. Each sweep or flick sent another bolt of desire through her, turning the temperature back up a notch. She reached one hand down and dug her fingers into his hair, and held on to the wall with her other hand. Another gasp left her when he eased a single long finger into her core and sucked her bead in time with the first thrust of his finger.

Hell.

Angels shouldn't be so wicked.

Not that she was about to file a complaint.

Einar licked her again, circling her nub and sending her out of her mind. She breathed hard, clinging to the wall and him to anchor herself. Her hand slipped from his head and she groaned and blindly reached for him.

Her fingers hit something soft and warm.

His wing.

She gripped it and the guttural moan that left his lips sent a sharp thrill through her, together with the way he buried his face deeper into her, until she felt as though he was going to devour her.

Tightness built inside her, the warmth pooling in her abdomen and swirling there, coiling into a ball of energy that had her writhing against Einar's tongue, seeking release.

He pulled his finger out of her, grasped her hips and stood.

In one swift, hard move, he plunged his cock into her, tearing a gasp from her throat.

Her eyes shot wide and she moaned when he withdrew and thrust back in.

She clasped his shoulder with one hand and his wing with the other. He kissed her hard, stealing her breath away, swallowing each of her moans, and moved inside her, rough and possessive, pinning her to the wall. Her eyes closed and she held on to him in every way possible, desperately trying to anchor herself as he went to war on her.

She wrapped her legs around his waist and he clutched her bottom, bringing her down onto his cock each time he pumped her, his movements fast and hungry. He groaned into her mouth and then kissed back down to her throat.

Taylor followed suit, kissing his strong jaw and neck, tasting his salty skin and warmth, taking his earthiness into her. She couldn't stop herself from satisfying the urge to bite him, sinking her teeth into his shoulder. It tensed beneath her teeth and he grunted as he thrust harder, filling her roughly and slamming his pelvis against hers.

Ripples of pleasure echoed through her each time his body brushed her bead and she shook in his arms, clenching around him and reaching for her climax. It was swift to come, crashing over her in waves so strong that she could barely catch her breath.

Einar thrust harder, plunging deep into her, and she moaned when he dug his fingers into her bottom, clutching her so violently that it hurt. She didn't care. She could only focus on the feel of him inside her, moving against her, filling her with his delicious body. She could only thrill at how strong he was, holding her at his mercy, sending her soaring again.

She pulsed around him, pleasure still chasing through her, and moaned softly as she tensed her muscles until he choked out a groan against her throat and shuddered to a halt inside her, his cock throbbing with release.

He breathed hard in her ear and kissed her throat, tender and soft now as he slowly came back down to Earth. She rested her head on his shoulder and held on to him, all of her energy draining from her as she came down with him.

Deep in her heart, she believed in what he had said when they had first made love.

Nothing that felt so right could ever be wrong.

They were made for each other.

An angel and a demon.

Nothing would change that.

She wouldn't let it.

CHAPTER 13

Light floated into Einar's mind at the feel of Taylor's soft lips pressing a kiss against his cheek. He reached for her as sleep drifted away but she was gone. He sighed and listened to her quietly walking across the bedroom as he stretched out in the warm double bed.

He couldn't remember a time he had felt so content and relaxed.

Not even his nightmarish fight with the demon and consequent narrow escape from death bothered him now.

Taylor had chased away that fear and the horror of that memory, soothing it with kisses and words of affection whispered against his skin during their lovemaking.

Another sigh escaped him and he opened his eyes and stared at the ceiling of the pale room. Bright sunlight filtered in through the two tall sash windows to his right, filling the room with a warm glow. The sun was close to setting. This was his favourite time of day but it had never felt like this.

He had never felt so happy.

He had never realised that he had felt so alone.

Taylor's company, her presence in his life, had given him more purpose than hunting had ever done. He lived to see her smile and hear her sweet voice.

Even when she was murdering a song.

He smiled at the sound of her poor singing. He didn't know the tune, but it was upbeat and carried a note of cheerfulness that made his smile widen. Perhaps she was happy too. She certainly felt it.

The underlying current of bliss had even been there this morning when they had bid a rather awkward farewell to Villandry and the nurse at the demon medical centre.

Villandry's expression had been as black as night and there had been malice in his red eyes as he had stared at Einar. Taylor had come under his scrutiny too but she had been quick to make an escape out into the sunlight where the vampire couldn't follow.

She had blushed several amusing shades of crimson when Einar had joined her on the quiet street. He had been sorely tempted to tease her but had let it go. He didn't care that the vampire had heard them making love.

In fact, he was glad that he had.

Now Villandry knew that Taylor was his.

Einar hoped they didn't need the vampire to help them again. He was sure the fiend would attempt to provoke him by flirting with Taylor or bringing up their past.

That thought crowded his mind together with others about the club and what had happened on the rooftop, bringing reality crashing back in to ruin what had been a dreamlike few hours alone with Taylor.

Another of the demons was dead but one remained—the one who had managed to sink his claws into Einar.

Would that demon believe that he had killed him?

Einar wasn't sure if that would work to their advantage at all, but he hoped it would make the demon more bold, maybe a little reckless if luck was with him. If the male thought he was dead, he might be open about travelling around, might come out of hiding and give Einar a chance to hunt him down and capture him.

Desire for revenge swept through him like wildfire, fierce and consuming, but he tamped it down. Two of the demons had already died. He needed the third so Heaven could question him and get to the bottom of the plot these three demons had been involved in with Commander Amaer.

There had to be a reason that an angel had been working with them.

Was it something to do with the Euphoria that Taylor had spoken of?

She had sounded as though she hadn't approved, and so had the boss of Cloud Nine. Was it considered taboo in the demon world? He had hunted amongst the mortals and demons for centuries and had never heard of it.

Even if it wasn't anything to do with Euphoria, he needed to report it to his commanders. He couldn't allow demons to run a club designed to enslave mortals and harm them for the sake of giving pleasure to the wretched creatures who had poisoned them.

He mulled over what Taylor had told him. She didn't suspect they were killing humans at the new club where Euphoria was being peddled, and as little as he wanted to admit it, because it gave him less reason to burn the place to the ground, he believed they weren't murdering the mortals.

If they were, humans would realise something was wrong with the club and would stay away.

Something *was* happening though.

A hundred human bodies had been destroyed in the warehouse event a few years ago and the shadowy demons and an angel had been responsible for it. Something had killed those mortals. He just wasn't sure what. All he had to show for his investigation was two dead demons and no answers.

He clenched his fists and glared at the ceiling.

If only he had been able to examine one of the human bodies. Maybe it would have given him clues as to what had happened to cause so much death. The demons had incinerated the evidence though, the fire so hot that all that remained at the factory were ashes and fragments of bones. None of it had yielded any evidence to assist the investigation.

Had they been hiding something or just protecting themselves from angelic intervention?

Amaer had brought the demons' activities to the attention of Heaven by calling Lukas to the warehouse and pinning the crime on him.

Had it been part of their plan, or had that caused tension between the demons and Amaer?

He rubbed the bridge of his nose and closed his eyes, frowning as his head ached.

Heaven had looked over all the evidence and had come up with nothing. He wasn't going to do any better without apprehending the last demon and bringing it in for interrogation.

They had to come up with a plan and a way to get them into the club unnoticed, or at least close enough that they could lure the final demon out again. He was sure the wretch had returned there, possibly even lived in the hellhole. Damn, the fiend might even run it.

Einar tossed the bedclothes aside, swung his legs over the edge of the bed and stood.

He went to wave a hand over himself to call his armour and then thought the better of it and called just his dark brown loincloth instead. Calling his armour from where it rested on the couch in the other room would drain some of his power and he needed to save it in case there was another fight between him and the demon tonight. It was strong and he couldn't risk it injuring him again. He might not survive this time, so for once he would manually put his armour on later.

Besides, there were advantages to wearing little clothing.

He stalked across the bedroom and out into the living area of the hotel suite.

Taylor whirled to face him, her back to one of the tall sash windows, a smile lighting up her face as her eyes landed on him. Whatever she had been about to say fled those tempting lips and her blue eyes darkened as they raked over him.

The evening light highlighted her curves and the fact she wore only black panties and a matching spaghetti strap top, both of them tight against her body, revealing it to him.

A groan rolled up his throat as he prowled towards her.

Her gaze fell to his body, heat chasing in its wake as she took him in. Her lips parted and her tongue swept across them.

He stalked towards her, drawn by her beauty and the soft but hungry look in her eyes. Maybe they could plan their attack later. Right now, he had far more interesting things on his mind.

Like making love to her again.

Now that things were out in the open between them, and they were both aware of the growing feelings of the other, he couldn't deny his desire for her. It went beyond lust and hunger, deeper than love itself. He needed her so much that he could only think of protecting her and keeping her safe, of keeping her by his side forever.

A stab of cold chilled his heart.

Forever wasn't an option.

It was impossible to do his duty and remain with her. He knew that. What they had was beautiful and something he didn't want to give up though. There had to be a way.

The voice at the back of his mind said that he knew there was only one way for them to be together.

Was he strong enough to do such a thing?

She reached out to him, a smile on her face, and then it fell away and fear filled her eyes.

Einar frowned.

The window exploded.

He shielded his face with his arms.

Taylor screamed.

It tore through him, chilled his blood and then set it on fire.

He lowered his arm, his heart beating fast against his ribs, sending adrenaline rushing through his body. Glass littered the floor and hung from the broken white window frame. His gaze darted around, searching for Taylor.

She was gone.

Einar ran to the window, over broken glass that sliced into his feet, and leaned out, searching for her. It took him a moment to spot her. A young man dressed in black was carrying her, his dark scaly wings beating the air as he lifted with her, rising up above the rooftops.

The demon.

Taylor struggled in his grip, flailing and kicking at him, but the man only tightened his hold on her.

"Taylor!" Einar stepped up on the window ledge and launched himself out into the wide street.

His wings burst from his back so fast it hurt and he beat them before he could fall into the road below and shot after her and the demon.

The demon looked back at him, a shock of bright red hair covering one eye, and grinned to reveal pointed teeth. He dug his fingers deep into her arms. Taylor shrieked again.

Einar set his jaw and flew after her, determined to save her from the demon. He wouldn't let the bastard harm her. He would protect her as he had silently promised, would uphold that vow no matter what happened to him.

A dark jagged line appeared in front of the demon and his heart hitched at the sight of it, panic flooding him. It split in two and grew, widening and opening, black filling the hole in the centre. By the time the demon reached it, it was large enough for him to pass through.

He disappeared into the darkness with Taylor.

Einar flew faster, his wings furiously beating the chilly air, and stretched out his hand, desperate to make it through and follow the demon to the other side. He pushed harder, gritted his teeth and ignored the burn of exertion in his wings.

He had to reach Taylor.

He had to save her.

The portal came within reach.

Shrank and winked out of existence right in front of him.

He stopped in mid-air, staring at the point where the portal had been.

Fury burned through him, blazing so hot he couldn't contain it as the thought of Taylor at the mercy of the demon tormented him. He threw his arms out at his sides, flung his head back and cursed the sky.

The world trembled below him and dark clouds gathered above. Screams filled his ears and car alarms blared. He breathed hard, fighting his desire to unleash his power and trying to purge his hunger for violence.

It was difficult as images of the demon torturing Taylor filled his mind, tore growls from his lips and had darkness bleeding into the edges of his soul.

Only the thought that she wouldn't want him to succumb to the black needs, wouldn't want him to endanger himself like that when she had come so close to losing him once already, gave him the strength to claw back control little by little, gathering enough to calm himself.

The sky lightened again and the earth stilled.

Einar stared in the direction of the club.

The demon would pay for taking Taylor.

He called his armour to him. The rich brown plates edged with dull gold appeared one by one on his body. His breastplate moulded over his chest and his back. His vambraces encased his forearms, and his boots and greaves protected his feet and shins. The pointed slats around his hips were the last to form. He closed his eyes and called again, and his sword appeared at his waist.

His hand went straight to it and he drew the blade.

It gleamed in the light of the setting sun.

He gripped it and fought to curb his anger.

It was impossible when he knew that Taylor was in danger.

Heaven called him. Orders to report to court.

Einar ignored them.

They could punish him later.

Right now, he had a demon to kill and the woman he loved to save.

He plummeted towards the street and then beat his wings at the last moment and shot along the road just above the vehicles, invisible to human eyes. He took each corner sharply, never slowing for a moment, zigzagging through the city towards the club in Soho where they had sent Villandry.

The demon would be there.

This ended tonight and he would be the victor.

CHAPTER 14

Einar wrestled with himself as he flew towards the club, his blood on fire with the need to save Taylor and make the demon pay for taking her from him. The urge to kill him was strong, but he fought against it, clinging to his tattered control because he needed the male alive. Not for the sake of completing his investigation, his mission on Earth, but for the sake of protecting Taylor.

And maybe himself too.

He couldn't report to Heaven's Court and declare that he had not only fallen for a demoness but he had killed all of those responsible for the deaths of the humans. If he captured the demon, they might be lenient in their punishment and they might not make her a target for another angel to take down.

It was going to be difficult though. The hunger to kill pounded inside him like a war drum, driving him to obey it. Denying it was going to take all of his strength.

The journey to the club passed in a blur as he fought to retain control, almost as desperate to make that happen as he was to save Taylor.

Einar landed hard on the quiet road outside the dark brick building, breathing heavily as he furled his tawny wings against his back and scanned the area with his senses.

Nothing on the outside. No watchers or guards tonight. The demon wanted it one on one. The demon might be stronger than him, but he wasn't about to let the wretch defeat him.

The sign above the entrance to the club was unlit.

Einar walked to the door and pressed his ear to it. There were voices on the other side, muffled and indistinct. A man. The demon? He couldn't hear Taylor. Was she alright? He took a deep breath, trying to catch her scent. He couldn't smell any blood but her perfume laced the air. She was here.

He opened the door a crack, enough that he could hear the voices clearer.

"You honestly believe he will come for you?" The male voice held a snide and derisive note that had Einar itching to burst into the room and prove him wrong.

The sound of footsteps echoed in the dark.

"He'll come and he'll kick your fucking arse when he does." Taylor.

She grunted a moment later and her pain echoed inside him. He tightened his grip on his sword. She was right. He was going to kick the demon's arse for her. He was going to kill the bastard for hurting her.

No. He couldn't kill the male. As much as he wanted to destroy him, he needed the demon alive.

"I told you to shut up." A loud smack filled the large room.

The echo of pain he picked up from Taylor grew stronger.

Einar's blood burned. He flexed his fingers around the hilt of his sword, on the verge of bursting in and slaughtering the demon, and stilled when he sensed her calling to him.

Only this time she wasn't asking him to come to her.

She was telling him to stay away.

Conflicting feelings rang through the muddled voice. Only part of her wanted him to keep away and leave her to the demon. The other half was screaming out for him to save her.

He wasn't going to abandon her.

He would save her because it was all he could do.

He loved her.

"This'll keep you quiet," the demon said and Taylor cried out again.

The smell of blood filled the air.

Her blood.

The demon had cut her. Had he used his claws and infected her with toxin? Fury rippled through Einar and he ground his teeth.

Taylor snarled.

The demon struck her again, the sound filling the room, and spat, "If I had known you were trash I wouldn't have bothered to pick you up. That bastard won't come for you. *Trash*."

Einar had heard enough.

He kicked the door in, sending it flying off its hinges, and swept through the club, knocking dark wooden tables and red velvet chairs with his wings in the process.

The demon barely dodged his blade. He lunged to his left and Einar's eyes narrowed on the fiend when he grabbed Taylor and twisted with her, using her as a shield. Her head drooped and Einar ran his gaze over her, assessing the damage. Her lip was split on the right side and her cheek was bruised and black. Similar dark marks peppered her bare legs.

There were long cuts across her chest too.

Claw marks?

Her eyes closed and then opened again and her head jerked up. She looked at the hands clutching her arms, awareness washed across her face and her eyes widened, and she struggled against her captor.

Grimaced when the demon twisted her arm behind her back.

Einar readied his sword.

The demon pressed his claws close to Taylor's jugular and grinned, his sharp teeth bright white in the blue lights of the club.

"I didn't think you would come for her. I had planned to drug her and let the boys loose on her to piss you off, but once I realised what she was, I was bitterly disappointed. But here you are, come to rescue this half-breed hunter bitch. Maybe I should have toyed with her after all, fucked her up a little, but I find her repulsive." The young man's face twisted in disgust. "I am surprised that you don't."

Einar checked Taylor again. She was wide awake now, her eyes enormous and full of fear, fixed towards the demon's hand against her throat. Tears lined her lashes and tore at him. It killed him to see his beautiful, confident and sassy little demoness so afraid.

"Taylor. Look at me, Taylor," Einar said and her gaze slid to meet his. She swallowed and her eyebrows furrowed. She had been so strong until now, almost reckless in her fearlessness, that seeing her so afraid made how much danger she was in hit home. He wanted to free her and give her reason to feel safe again, but he couldn't do that with the demon's claws poised over her artery. All he could do was try to make her feel safe with a promise that he intended to keep. "Are you alright?"

She nodded almost imperceptibly.

"That's good. Keep still and keep calm. Just breathe slowly and try not to panic. It will slow the rate of poisoning from the toxin." Einar held her gaze, breathing slowly himself so she would follow suit. He heard her heartbeat start to level out as she took long deep breaths and began to relax. "I will get you out of here. I will not let anything happen to you. You understand?"

She nodded again. He smiled at her.

The demon made a retching sound.

Einar's gaze narrowed and slid to him.

"Let her go. This is between us. It has nothing to do with her." He held his hand out to Taylor, hoping the demon would let her go but knowing that it wasn't going to be so easy.

The young man chuckled and shook his head, his red hair shifting with it.

He grinned. "I think I prefer that she is between us. You seem rather irritated tonight and I want protection while I cut you a deal."

"A deal?" Einar couldn't believe what he was hearing.

He took a step towards the demon where he stood on the dance floor. The demon disappeared with Taylor and reappeared on the empty black stage.

He glared at Einar and bit out, "Stay there, like a good boy, or I make your bitch into my marionette. I haven't tested it, but I think the combination of my blood and toxin would be enough to control another demon. Let's keep this civilised, just as it was with that other angel."

"Amaer," Einar spat the name out with disgust.

The demon nodded. "He was quick to sign his name when I offered him power and money, and a chance to play."

"In exchange for what?" Einar couldn't let the chance slip him by.

He had to know what had tempted Commander Amaer to join the demons and work with them against the mortals.

"Something only an angel can do." The demon ghosted his claws down Taylor's throat, his gaze dropping to her and wrenching a growl from Einar's lips.

The male looked up at him and grinned, flashing fangs again. The bastard liked having power over him. Well it wasn't going to last. He was going to find a way to get Taylor out of his hands and then he was going to deal with him and show him who had the real power.

He frowned at the demon, playing along. "I will need a little more information than that. Your offer isn't very tempting... Taylor said this club dealt in Euphoria."

He glanced at her again, checking her vitals. The poison was taking effect. He had to get her away and to safety. Duty warred with love inside him. He couldn't surrender this chance to capture the demon and get information on why Amaer had been working with them, but he couldn't risk Taylor's life either.

"Euphoria isn't illegal." The demon tilted Taylor's head up and she squeaked and stiffened when his claw nicked her throat. "Didn't she tell you that?"

Taylor hadn't mentioned it but it didn't matter. This demon was involved in something that was illegal and Einar was going to find out what it was. He couldn't question the demon directly about Amaer. It was better that he went along with the demon and got him to talk. He didn't have much time though. It wouldn't be long before the toxin started to take hold in Taylor.

"I don't care what's legal and what isn't." He risked another step towards the demon and straightened to his full height, looking down at the male. "I thought you were offering me a deal?"

"Money, power, anything you want... I'll even throw her in to sweeten it." The demon let Taylor's head fall forwards again.

Einar forced himself to remain rooted to the spot. He couldn't attack. He had to wait until the right moment. Taylor was doing well and keeping calm. As long as she didn't try anything, she would be safe for now.

"All I ask is that you cut me some slack and help out occasionally." The male smiled charmingly. "After all, it's just a few humans. Demons need entertainment too but sometimes they go a little too far."

Einar frowned again. Just a few humans? There had been at least a hundred in the warehouse and no one knew how many had died in the years since that night. Even one mortal life was too many.

"I try to keep them in check and run a clean business but sometimes there's... accidental possessions." The demon shrugged.

Fury blazed through Einar again, burning in his blood.

Possession.

That was why the demons had needed an angel. If a human died whilst possessed, a record appeared in the list of the dead stating such and Heaven sent an investigation team to the location.

There was a treaty between Heaven and Hell that forbade possessions.

Amaer had been exorcising the humans before they died, so none of them registered as unusual deaths. He had been protecting the sick business these demons were running, letting them get away with breaking the law.

And for what?

Money, power, and the chance to twist a mortal to his control and treat them as a slave.

Einar had heard enough.

He shifted his grip on his sword, stared the demon down and coldly said, "No deal."

Before the demon could move, Einar was beside him, gripping the hand the demon had at Taylor's throat. He twisted the demon's arm and pushed Taylor forwards.

She stumbled and fell off the stage, landing in a heap on the dance floor. He didn't have time to check on her. He ducked when the demon swiped at him with his other hand and brought his knee up hard into the wretch's stomach. The demon snarled and Einar grabbed him, twisted and hurled him across the room. He slammed into the dark bar near the entrance of the club, landing on his side on the black floor.

Einar leaped down off the stage and grabbed Taylor, pulling her up into his arms and cradling her close to him. He scanned the room for the demon, coiled tight and ready for the male to attack him.

He was gone. Not good.

Einar turned with Taylor held tight against him, shielding her with his left wing as she gripped his breastplate. His focus kept switching between her and the room. He tried to keep it on the room but it was impossible when Taylor was beginning to feel weak on his senses. The toxin was spreading through her, killing her. He had to get her to somewhere he could heal her.

He spun on the spot, bringing his sword up at the same time, and blocked the demon. The male grinned and leaped back. He had changed again, shedding his human skin to reveal the dark scaly demon he truly was. Thin lips peeled back to reveal equally dark sharp teeth and his black wings stretched out, making the room look small.

He beat them and shot towards Einar.

It was easy to dodge the attack in such a confined space.

Einar unfurled his tawny feathered wings and flew across the dance floor towards the exit. He landed when he reached the cluttered chairs and tables, swiftly carrying Taylor towards the other end of the room. He set her down behind the dark wooden bar and checked her over.

"Stay here. I will be right back." He touched her cheek and grimaced.

It was blazing beneath his fingers.

Beads of sweat dotted her brow and she looked up at him with dull eyes that had him lingering, unable to leave her. He leaned in and pressed a kiss to her forehead. He didn't want to leave her, even when he knew that he had to in order to save her. He needed to deal with the demon.

His heart whispered that he needed to stay with her. His touch alone would ease her pain and slow the spread of toxin, and he could use his power to draw it out of her.

She weakly lifted her hand, slapped it against his chest and pushed him backwards, a silent order that threatened to break his heart.

He didn't want to leave her, but she was right and he had to go. She was strong. She wouldn't give up. She would keep fighting the poison until he returned and healed her.

He gripped his sword as he drew back, lingered a moment to steal one more look at her, and stepped out into the room again, coming to face the demon.

The creature snarled and shifted towards him, his talons flexing at his sides. The lights above the stage illuminated his black wings as he stretched them, turning them blue.

Einar held his ground. The demon wouldn't attack that way again. He was clever enough to know that he didn't stand a chance if he flew at him.

The bar and tables crowded where Einar stood, leaving only a narrow strip of floor open. Not enough room to fly into or out of without colliding with the furniture and being slowed down by it.

He raised his hand, calling what little energy he could afford to expend without draining himself. He needed to conserve his power so he had enough to heal Taylor.

He flung his hand forwards, sending thin spears of light at the shadowy demon as it shrieked at him. They flew in a stream, one after the other, and the demon disappeared and reappeared, dodging and snarling all the while.

He didn't relent. He sent hundreds of them at the demon, filling the room with white light. The bastard couldn't evade them all. One or two would hit him eventually, and even if he did manage to avoid them, he was using up his energy by disappearing. He would be tiring.

Einar dodged when the demon appeared right in front of him and he threw his hand out towards him. A single shaft of light grazed the demon's cheek, sliced through the dark membrane of his wing and embedded itself in the far wall.

The demon shrieked again, the sound hurting Einar's ears, and his lizard-like yellow eyes narrowed as he hissed. He disappeared and reappeared right behind Einar, leaving him no chance to evade the male's attack.

Talons raked down his left wing, ripping a bellow from his lips as he arched forwards and pain blazed through his bones.

"Einar," Taylor called out to him and the demon's head snapped around towards her.

Einar shook off the pounding in his skull and focused in an attempt to contain the toxin entering his bloodstream. It would be slower to act now that he had been exposed to it and had survived, his body building some immunity, but it would still kill him far quicker than it would Taylor.

The demon lumbered towards her.

Einar sprinted after him as he finally shut down the pain and reached the male just in time to grab his arm as he swiped at her. The demon's talons stopped close to her face and she curled up into a ball with her hands over her head.

"Keep down." Einar gritted his teeth as a fresh wave of pain washed through him.

His senses dulled as it receded and he battled to keep his focus.

He yanked the demon back and wrapped his hand around the male's throat. Sharp scales grated against his palm but he tightened his grip, ignoring the pain it caused him to do so. He growled and threw the demon across the room.

The male hit the stage, bending backwards over it, and slumped to the floor.

Einar shot across the room, using his power to speed him towards the demon before he could get back onto his feet. He grabbed the male's throat again, hauled him into the air, choking him, and slammed him down onto the stage. He pinned him there, throttling him.

The demon's yellow eyes shone up from his black scaly face as he snarled and struggled, kicking and scratching at Einar but catching only his armour.

Einar clenched his jaw and punched the demon, and then hit him again. The sound of Taylor's shallow breathing and racing heart drove him on. He beat the wretched male, striking him until his face was as damaged as hers was.

It wasn't enough.

Anger ripped through him, violence demanding satisfaction, and he obeyed. He closed both hands around the demon's throat, tightened his grip on it and bashed the back of his skull against the stage until the black painted wood split beneath him.

The demon snarled, a line of dark blood trickling down his cheek and coating his sharp teeth as a glistening patch formed on the wood.

Einar didn't relent.

Was so caught up in dealing payback to the demon, satisfying his lust for violence, that he didn't see the male move.

Fire seared his bare stomach, the scent of his own blood joining that of the demon's in the air as the male's talons raked over his flesh.

The effect of the toxin was instantaneous.

His head spun, his heart hammering hard against his chest and his body weakening as it seized hold of him.

The demon kicked him backwards and he fell onto the floor of the club, his wings bent painfully beneath him.

He tried to block and defend himself, but his limbs refused to cooperate, his head spinning so fast he felt sick as the world pitched and turned. The demon leaped on him, digging his claws into Einar's throat and choking him. Awareness trickled through him, a sensation he should do something.

But he didn't have the strength to break free.

It bled from him as the demon grinned maliciously, his yellow eyes narrowing with it, and tore at his wings.

He roared in agony, pain radiating through him, stealing his senses and remaining strength as the demon ripped at them, claws slashing and tearing feathers away, scattering them around him.

A new fire burned inside him, a need to survive. He had to protect Taylor. If he failed here, she would be next. The demon would torture her and kill her too.

He couldn't let that happen.

He gritted his teeth and called on all of his power, mustering the last of his strength.

The demon snarled and bit Einar's shoulder, razor-sharp teeth slicing through the leather straps of his chest armour, and he cried out again. He raised his hands, fighting against the weakness invading his body, and pressed them against the demon's chest.

The demon froze and looked down at them, a flicker of fear entering his eyes. Grinned when nothing happened.

No use. Einar didn't even have the energy to blast the demon off him.

The bastard knew it. His sharp grin widened.

And then his face went slack and his eyes widened, the thin line of his pupils stretching until black drowned out the yellow. Blood bubbled from his black lips and dripped onto Einar's breastplate, and he followed the trail of it, his own eyes widening as he saw the tip of the blade protruding from the demon's chest.

His gaze snapped to Taylor where she stood over both him and the demon, her hands clutching his sword as it speared the demon's back.

"That's for calling me bitch," she bit out and then twisted the sword, ripping a pained grunt from the demon.

Her eyes slipped shut but she opened them again. Her heartbeat was off the scale, thundering in his ears as he struggled to focus on her, sending a cold wave through him that left him feeling hollow inside.

The poison was killing her. She shouldn't have moved.

Einar wanted to tell her that but before he could utter a word, a bright white light engulfed them all.

He fought against it and reached out towards Taylor, fear pounding through him for a different reason now. He wouldn't let Heaven have her. He wouldn't let them take her from him.

It didn't matter that it was forbidden.

It only mattered that he loved her and she loved him.

The beam of light lifted them into the air.

Taylor reached for him too, fighting the restrictive force of the light as her face twisted in agony. Her fingers touched his and he smiled at her, desperate to reassure her.

Nothing would happen to her.

He would see to that.

He would fight Heaven itself to protect her.

CHAPTER 15

Taylor wrapped her arms around herself to keep the chill off. Her fingertips brushed the scars on her thick leather jacket and she stroked the badly sewn ridges. A smile touched her lips but disappeared a moment later when thoughts of how she had met Einar all those weeks ago made her heart ache.

It hurt whenever she thought about him, which was all the damned time.

Would she ever see him again?

She lowered her head and continued through the cemetery, losing focus as she thought about Einar. The big oaf. She smiled and gave a short but melancholy laugh.

She missed him.

She hadn't seen him since the light had taken them to Heaven along with the last of the demons that Einar had been hunting.

He had tried to stay with her but angels with long blue spears and blue armour had separated them and dragged her away through the bright white corridors.

They had taken Einar the other way.

She had asked about him, begged the medical staff tending to her to tell her whether he was alright and that he wasn't going to die from the toxin the demon had infected them with.

No one had spoken a word to her.

They had healed her and then she had fallen asleep and awoken in the hotel suite.

Alone.

Taylor shivered at the memory and the ceaseless pain she had felt since that night. She wanted to see him again. She needed to know if he was alright even if they couldn't be together anymore, even if Heaven forbid it and they had to let their love go.

She just needed to see him one last time.

Even if it broke her heart.

She silently berated herself for being so weak and for latching on to such a hopeless dream.

Einar was gone.

Her heart was already broken.

She sighed and frowned at the wet grass. Cold fingers of wind caressed her face, freezing it. Autumn was turning towards winter and soon she would have to give up waiting for him.

She couldn't ignore her duty as a hunter anymore.

There were bills to pay, a city to protect, and her life was a mess.

Everyone was talking about her. She had gone to Cloud Nine when Einar had disappeared and the regulars had met her with distrust. Even Villandry wasn't speaking to her.

Taylor looked at her dark hilly surroundings, at the tombstones that swept out in all directions on the bleak landscape, and held herself a little tighter.

The city stretched into the distance before her, yellow lights twinkling like stars.

Before she had met Einar, this had been her favourite view of London. Now she could only think of how magical the city had looked from his strong arms as they had flown above it.

Damn it.

He wasn't coming back and nursing her broken heart wasn't getting her anywhere.

She was stronger than this and she had a job to do.

Several demons had come and gone, terrorising lesser demons in her city, and she hadn't intervened. It was time she picked herself up, pulled her shit together, and started taking care of business again.

It was time that she showed everyone that she was the same fearless and dangerous woman she had been before she had fallen in love with an angel.

In fact, she was stronger because of it.

She clenched her fists and straightened her back, feeling the resolve as it flowed through her. She was going to protect this city. She was going to keep moving forwards in life, and maybe one day she would meet Einar again.

And she would give him hell for leaving her.

The city lights blinked and flickered. Her city. It was safe from Euphoria for now, but there was still so much work for her to do. She would protect the mortals, and watch over them. She would carry on, unafraid of what the future held because she was strong enough to face anything now.

It was her love for Einar, and his love for her, and the memory of their time together that would always live in her heart, that gave her the strength to continue.

It made her fearless.

She jumped and screamed when someone grabbed her from behind, their arms tight bands of steel across her chest, pinning hers to her sides. She kicked and struggled as they lifted her feet off the ground and managed to reach the knife she had sheathed against her right hip.

Taylor raised it as her attacker twisted her in their arms to face them and stopped just short of stabbing his shoulder.

She blinked.

Her heart thundered painfully in her throat.

Reality slowly sunk in and she frowned.

"Where the hell have you been?" She cuffed him across the side of the head.

Hard.

He set her down, glaring at her as he rubbed his right temple.

"Hardly the welcome I had expected." Einar's deep voice made her insides flip and tremble but she refused to let it affect her. Not even his charming smile was going to weaken her this time. "Where's my kiss?"

It wreaked havoc on her as it curled his sensual lips. Utterly destroyed her and tore down all her defences.

Damn him.

Was it always going to be like this? Was she always going to be little more than a moon-eyed girl around him? Just as she had found her strength again too.

His smile widened and he was devastating in his handsomeness as banked heat filled his earthy eyes and beckoned her.

She cursed again when she found herself compelled to leap into his arms and kiss him.

To Hell with it.

She had already made a fool of herself by screaming at the top of the lungs when he had grabbed her. She wasn't going to make herself look any weaker than she already did if she wrapped him in her arms and kissed him into oblivion just as she wanted to.

She knocked the smile off his face by throwing herself at him.

He caught her, his strong arms wrapping tightly around her waist, and she crushed his lips with a kiss so fierce that she could barely breathe. Damn, it felt good to be back in his arms again and to feel all his love for her as he kissed her.

She slowed down and let him take the lead, loving the way his tongue gently traced hers and their lips softly played against each other.

Her insides lightened, the warmth of her emotions chasing away the chill of the night and all the ones that had come before this moment.

Taylor broke the kiss and held him, pressing her cheek to his as those lonely nights caught up with her. "You didn't come back."

He sighed and kissed her jaw, her neck, and then his grip on her tightened, his hands splayed out against her back, and she felt sure he would never let her go again.

"I am here now. I am sorry it took me so long." The sound of his voice was heavenly, whispered softly in the shell of her ear, his breath as teasing as his kiss had been.

She didn't want to let him go. Fear that he would disappear again washed through her and she held him closer, clinging to his dark shirt.

Shirt?

She frowned and looked down at his back.

No wings.

He wasn't wearing his armour either.

She wriggled so much that he released her, setting her back down on the wet grass. She cast her gaze over him, frowning all the while. He was dressed as a mortal, wearing black jeans and a shirt, and black boots.

Why was he dressed as a mortal?

Her eyes widened.

Tears filled them when she realised why he no longer looked like an angel. She couldn't bring herself to believe that he had done such a thing, tried to convince herself that she was reading into his appearance and he was just undercover as a mortal, but the hurt in his eyes said that her suspicion was correct.

"They kicked you out because of me." Those words fell like lead in the darkness, slamming into the earth and shaking the tears from her eyes.

She couldn't breathe as she looked at him, saw all the pain just beneath the surface, and knew it was because of her. She had never wanted to hurt him.

Taylor hated everyone in Heaven and the thought that they had taken Einar's wings from him.

She hated herself.

"No," Einar husked and she drew in a sharp shaky breath when he touched her cheek.

His fingers caressed it and then he flattened his palm against it and raised her head as though he wanted to keep her eyes on his. His hand was warm against her face and she brought hers up and covered it, holding it there.

He smiled and she saw all the love in it and in his eyes, and watched as all the pain they held disappeared.

His voice dropped to a whisper. "They gave me a choice, Taylor. Either I gave you up or I gave up my wings."

She leaned into his touch, the beauty of what he had done for her stealing her voice and her heart, making it difficult to breathe as her love for him overwhelmed her, beating in every fibre of her being, running in her veins like blood and filling her with peace and happiness.

She didn't know the words to thank him for making such a great sacrifice for her sake and the sake of their love. She wasn't sure there were any that were adequate enough, so all she could do was show him what this meant to her.

What he meant to her.

She wrapped her arms around his neck again and held him, her eyes closing and her heart swelling. His arms encircled her waist and he sighed against her neck, holding her against his broad chest.

"You didn't have to," she whispered and kissed his ear.

She threaded her fingers into his mousy short ponytail and then stroked his neck, savouring the warmth of him against her, hoping this would last forever.

Would he regret what he had done one day?

She had met fallen angels and knew how difficult it was for them to leave the world they had been born into and join the mortal one they had once protected. It was going to be a hard transition for Einar but she would be there every step of the way, giving her love to him and supporting him, forever. She would never stop thanking him for what he had done for her, for them, so they could be together.

"I did." He rubbed his cheek against hers and then took hold of her waist and pushed her back. He smiled into her eyes and brushed his thumb across her jaw. The affection in his gaze brought a blush to her cheeks. No one had ever looked at her with so much love before. "I had to, because I could not bear to be away from you and to see you suffering."

Had he been watching over her?

She couldn't decide which was worse—being alone and not knowing if they would ever see each other again, or being able to see her love and not being able to go to them.

Taylor kissed him, tasting him on her lips and breathing him in. Her warrior angel. They had been through so much together but she had never imagined it would turn out this way.

"You fell for me." Her eyes met his again.

His smile widened. "I fell for you in more than one way. I love you, Taylor."

She smiled from ear to ear as he lifted her off the ground, his hands on her backside. It didn't matter if she looked like a moon-eyed girl right now. No one was watching and the man that she was crazy about had just told her that he loved her.

Her.

A demon.

And she loved him.

An angel.

Or at least an ex-angel.

She kissed his cheek, pressed her hands against his broad shoulders, and looked down into his eyes.

"I love you." Her voice shook with those words. Einar smiled up at her. He had never looked as handsome as he did now, with his gaze on her and full of affection. She shook her head, her eyebrows furrowing. "But I never wanted it to come to this."

His smile held. "I know, but it was my choice, Taylor, and I will never regret it. I will never regret anything when it comes to you."

He kissed her again, brief and sweet, and she melted against him. She wanted more but couldn't shake the questions bubbling up inside her.

"What will you do now?" she murmured against his lips.

He broke away from her, his left eyebrow arching, and set her back on her feet.

So she was being practical when he was giving her those 'come get me' eyes that he had used so often on her, but they were in the middle of a cemetery and it was hardly the weather for making love in the open.

That would have to wait until she got him back to her place.

Right now, she wanted to stay in his arms and bask in his beauty and the fact he had come back to her.

"I have been watching you. You look as though you could use a hand keeping the demons in line." He shot her a cheeky grin as she frowned at him for questioning her skill in the hunting department. "Plus... I promised some old friends I would help them with a problem. Our first job together, all lined up. What do you know about witches?"

"They're not my specialty." She didn't miss the look in his eyes that said he was serious about them working together, and that this mission in particular was important to him. A job for old friends. "Is this for some angels?"

She wasn't sure she was ready to work with more angels, but she would do it for him.

He pulled a face. "Sort of... I was asked by them, but it's for someone else... someone we had thought was lost to us. It will not be easy."

She liked the sound of that even less. "Why won't it be easy?"

"The angel serves Hell now."

Those words fell on her like boulders, one after the other, and it took her a moment to shake the sudden bout of nerves that gripped her and free her of its hold.

She must have visibly tensed, because Einar frowned at her.

"You know demonic angels?" His dark gaze pierced hers.

She shrugged stiffly. "Don't ask."

When he looked as if he was going to, she silenced him with a kiss, savouring the way he instantly reacted, drawing her into his arms and holding her close to him as his mouth moved against hers. Damn, she had missed him too, wasn't sure she would be able to kiss him without it swiftly turning desperate for at least a few weeks.

"So, we will find this witch, help Rook and then we will find the next job. I am sure many would be happy to hire us as a team and we could hunt demons in the city whenever we do not have paying work." He was starting to sound like a mercenary.

She had never taken more than the occasional paying job, but he looked as if he was going to try to get them lined up one after the other, a steady income to go with a steady flow of dead demons in his wake. She supposed it shouldn't surprise her. He was a hunter angel after all.

She frowned.

Had been a hunter angel.

That hit her hard all over again.

124

"But you're mortal. You can't fight beside me. I won't risk you." It wasn't going to happen. Not again. She had been terrified when they had fought the demon, when he had been gravely injured and had looked close to death. He probably wasn't as vulnerable to demon toxin anymore, but he could be killed. She shook her head. "Demons are strong... you know that. Helping your friends is one thing... but hunting for a living... Einar—"

He pressed a finger to her lips.

"I am not mortal. I am fallen. I still have my powers, haven't forgotten how to use weapons or lost any of my impressive skills." He cracked a grin that had her heart fluttering and she glared at him to counter it, sure he had heard the effect he had on her when his dark eyes gained a twinkle. "I am still immortal... as strong as I used to be... but my status as an angel has been revoked, and they took my wings with it."

"Does that mean that there's a chance you can get them back? If you left me, would they reinstate your wings and make you an angel again?" She would do anything to help him regain them, even sacrifice her love for him and the future she had dreamed about. She would go through that pain to stop his suffering.

"Do not speak that way," Einar whispered and stroked her cheek, his gaze holding hers.

He hesitated.

She felt it in his touch and she frowned.

What wasn't he telling her?

He stared at the sky, as he had done the night he had received orders from Heaven.

Were they still speaking to him? Why would they speak to a fallen angel?

When his eyes dropped to hers again, he sighed. "I do not care if I never become an angel again. If my wings remain forever lost, I will not grieve, because I have you in my life. You are my everything, Taylor. The only thing I need."

"But," she said, sure that he was building towards confessing something important, and he frowned at her, a confused crinkle forming between his eyebrows. She pointed to the stars. "They're speaking to you. You had that funny distant look in your eyes that you get when there are voices in your head... so tell me what they're saying."

He sighed again. "There is a way for me to regain my wings, and it requires your help."

Other than leaving him, she wasn't sure what help she could be. She was a demon. It wasn't as though that was going to change, and she was certain that until it did, Heaven wasn't going to give Einar his wings back.

"I would prefer to discuss this somewhere more comfortable... say... in bed after we have become reacquainted, but you seem intent on questioning me here." Einar's expression turned pensive and serious. "Whether you agree or disagree, I will always love you. I need you to know that I am not going to ask you to do as Heaven desires. It does not matter to me whether they see you as demon or human. It only matters how I see you, and that I love you, and that you are mine."

"What do you mean, see me as demon or human?" Taylor frowned and looked up at the sky.

It wasn't possible that Heaven would see her as anything but demon. Black blood flowed in her veins as far as they were concerned, surely? She wasn't human.

"There is some debate in Heaven about your status. Hell has you recorded as demon at birth and Heaven has you recorded as human. They are arguing about it and have been since shortly before we were called to them. For now, Heaven's clerics are siding with Hell against us, but Heaven's Court has said that it will take into account that you were originally registered with Heaven as human and also your activity as a demon hunter. If you continue with your mission to protect humans from demons, they may confirm your status as a human."

"They're willing to overlook my demon blood?" She couldn't believe it.

Had Einar argued her case in court?

He had said that he didn't care whether Heaven saw her as human or demon, and she believed him. She just didn't believe that Heaven felt the same, but she was willing to do whatever it took to convince them that she was good, so Einar would regain his status.

"You do not have to do as they ask, Taylor. You have nothing to prove to them, or to anyone. I know who you are. I have seen it with my own eyes." He framed her face with his hands and stared down into her eyes, his filled with the honesty and love she was coming to adore seeing in them. "While there is a part of you who is demon, you have the heart and soul of a human, and have been working hard to keep mortals safe. Your courage and strength deserves recognition in Heaven without you needing to play their game. You have done your fellow humans a great service by risking your life to protect them."

Taylor had never really thought about her life like that. Hunting the bad demons, the ones who wanted to harm other demons and mortals, was just something that she had always felt she needed to do. She had never considered that it would ever curry her favour with the boss upstairs. She had always thought that everyone would see her as a demon regardless of what she did.

She stared into Einar's eyes.

Only he had never seen her as a demon.

He had told her once that she was just Taylor.

He didn't care about her demon or human blood. All he cared about was her.

Einar took hold of her hands, his fingers pressing into her palms. He stared down at them and pain cracked his voice when he spoke. "Do not feel you need to help me get my wings back, Taylor. It is a cruel game they are playing with you, and I do not care for it. I should never have tried to argue your case to them. It was wrong of me. I only wanted them to see that you had assisted me and that a true demon would never have done such a thing. I did not expect them to state that if you were truly human, you would protect your kind against the demons, and to offer me a choice. I either remained an angel and watched over you from above, with the chance that one day you would satisfy Heaven and they would decide you were human and we could be together... or I surrendered my wings and came to you."

"And you came to me." It touched her deeply, had her heart filling with love for him all over again, birthing a need to hold him and kiss him breathless.

"Not because of Heaven's plan for you to prove yourself. I came because I could not continue to watch you from afar and see you suffering. I knew that if I did not come to you, that you could lose hope and faith, and could turn away from your mission to protect humans and weaker demons from those who sought to hurt them. You could lose what happiness it had given you, and a part of yourself in the process." Einar squeezed her hands and his gaze met hers again. "I had to come to you and believe in our love for each other. I did not do it so you would one day convince Heaven to reinstate me. I did it so you would not be alone and so you would be happy again, and would continue with your mission... this time with me at your side."

"But I want to help you get your wings back." She slipped her left hand free of his and stroked his arm.

It was beautiful of him to try so hard to convince her that she shouldn't go along with what Heaven wanted, and she cherished the meaning behind his words. He believed that she was a good woman, one who made a difference in this world, and he loved her because of it.

He didn't want her to feel as though she had to prove herself, and she didn't.

She wasn't ashamed of her demon blood and she never would be, not when Einar loved her for who she was, regardless of where she had come from.

Heaven could see her how they wanted, but if it put an end to Einar's pain and meant they could be together as they had been before, she would go along with their game.

"I'll do whatever it takes, because I love you, and I know in my heart how important your duty is to you, because my duty is important to me too." She lifted her hand and stroked his cheek as his eyes searched hers, the beautiful golden flakes in them shifting slowly, swirling against the dark brown of his irises. There was pain brewing in his eyes, hurt that she could feel inside her. She wanted to vanquish it for him. "If someone took that away, I would be lost."

"I am lost," Einar whispered and hung his head, a deep sigh shifting his broad shoulders.

It hurt her to see her angel so forlorn and vulnerable. She cupped his cheek, smoothed her palm over it, and smiled when he looked at her through his lashes.

"You're not lost." She smiled up into his eyes. "You're still the same hunter I first met. Wings or no wings, you will never change. You're still the man I fell in love with."

One she would love forever.

He frowned when she sidled up to him and stroked her hands over his chest, savouring the feel of the hard compact muscles hidden beneath his black shirt. His dark gaze followed them and then met hers when she brushed her fingers up his neck and cupped his jaw.

If she could give him back his wings simply by continuing to hunt demons, she would do it every second of every day, never resting until he had regained them. She would do that for him because he loved her and had sacrificed so much to be with her.

She tiptoed and pressed her lips to his. He slanted his head and captured her mouth with his, his tongue stroking the seam of her lips and teasing her tongue into joining in. She closed her eyes and kissed him.

She would do it because she loved him.

Nothing would ever change that.

Not what others thought about them or how forbidden their relationship was. None of it mattered to her. All that mattered was that she was in love with him, and he was in love with her.

Where they had come from didn't mean anything.

It was where they were going to that counted.

And they would keep going forwards, hunting side by side, protecting the city and winning Einar's wings back one bad guy at a time.

Together.

The End

Read on for a preview of the next book in the Her Angel: Bound Warriors Series, Bound Angel!

BOUND ANGEL

The angel was back.

Rook stood on the precipice of a spire of black rock, the cragged and forbidding lands around him shimmering in the heat as it rose up from the fiery rivers snaking like lightning in all directions across the obsidian earth below him, illuminating the endless cavern of Hell.

He stared at the shadowy horizon in the direction of the Devil's fortress, not seeing the towering spikes of basalt that formed it. Not seeing anything. His gaze was turned inwards, focused on the strange sensation that swirled inside him whenever the angel set foot in Hell and dared to leave the plateau that overlooked the bottomless pit.

Rook had noticed it during their second encounter, when he had spotted the black-haired and onyx-winged angel scouting lands he had no right surveying. It was one thing for Heaven to have a contingent of angels posted on the plateau, where a silvery pool recorded the history of the mortal realm.

It was another thing entirely for one of his foul breed to venture out over the lands, flying where he didn't belong, trampling all over the Devil's territory.

Three times since then, Rook had dispatched the First Battalion to drive the male back into the area above the Devil's fortress.

Three times since then, the angel had gone quietly, retreating not just to the plateau but to a portal he could open between Hell and the mortal realm.

Which meant he was powerful.

Was that the reason Rook could sense him?

His eyes slipped shut and he inhaled slowly, filled his lungs with the sweet air of Hell and exhaled it all again, centring himself at the same time. The sensation grew stronger, swirled more violently inside him. Not in his gut, but behind the breastplate of his scarlet-edged black armour.

As he focused on it, it grew stronger still, setting him on edge. He shunned the unsettling emotion, refusing to let the angel rattle him again.

One time, the last time the angel had entered Hell, the commander of the First Battalion had been discussing business with their master and Rook had led the men in his stead, flying to meet the angel head on.

He had been determined to drive the male out of Hell just as his commander could, proving himself worthy of his position as his second, both to his commander and to the Devil. Rumours had it that the commander was falling out of favour for some reason, and Rook was damned if another would take his place as leader of the First Battalion when he had spent centuries working towards seizing control of the elite legion of angels under the Devil's command.

When he had found the intruder, the male had dared to speak to him, addressing him directly and calmly despite the threat of facing a hundred of Hell's most powerful angels.

He had mentioned a witch and something about helping her.

It had given Rook pause, and in turn that had left him cold, and furious. He had driven the angel out of Hell, pursuing him right to the plateau to ensure he left, because no creature of Heaven could sway him from his path.

The fiend had been trying to lure him from Hell. Rook was sure of it.

He just wasn't sure why the male wanted him to leave the realm of shadows and fire that was his home, his entire world.

His left hand fell to the red-edged obsidian vambrace that protected his right forearm and he clutched it as a different feeling rolled through him, one that always left him off balance, had him questioning things that in turn filled him with uncertainty—both about himself and the realm he loved so much.

The trouble was, those questions were fleeting, slipped through his fingers like smoke before they had fully formed, leaving him with a head full of muddled thoughts that had no meaning.

He focused to purge the sensation before it took hold, needing his mind in the present and sharp as a blade with the angel in his territory. He couldn't allow the tangled flow of questions and indistinct thoughts to strip him of his awareness today, weakening him.

The angel was coming.

To lure him through the portal into the mortal realm? For what purpose? To kill him?

It wouldn't be the first time that an angel of Heaven had lured one serving the Devil away from this realm to kill them, forcing them to return to Heaven.

Rook had no interest in dying, so he certainly had no interest in the angel or anything he had to say.

The bastard was persistent though.

He had returned quicker this time, and seemed to be heading swiftly in Rook's direction, as if he knew where he stood.

Impossible.

Hell was vast, blurred into shadows as far as the eye could see, no matter how far he flew. It was filled with angels like him too, ones who served the Devil, and countless demons. There was no way the male could single him out in the web of signatures. It was impossible.

Yet when Rook opened his eyes, a speck formed on the horizon, a glint of gold in a sea of red and black.

He rolled his head, stretching his neck, and flexed his fingers as he lowered his hands to his hips. He rested his left hand on the black hilt of the scarlet blade hanging at his waist and extended his crimson wings to ensure his feathers were lined up perfectly and they were ready for when he needed them. He casually furled them against his back as the angel drew closer, so they brushed the pointed slats of armour that protected his hips and the backs of his greaves.

His heart beat harder, muscles coiling beneath his skin as he waited.

Waited.

For a moment, it looked as if the angel would fly straight past him and then he diverted course, banking to his right and descending towards a flat section of the hill that rose up to Rook's left.

The male landed gracefully, neatened his ponytail with a steady hand, and gave a few more beats of his onyx wings before allowing them to settle against his back. He turned towards Rook, lifted his head and pinned him with bright blue eyes that glowed against the darkness of Hell.

Rook refused to move from his spire of rock.

He glared down at the male, his fingers tightening around the hilt of his sword. "Not learned your lesson yet?"

The male regarded him silently, no trace of emotion crossing his features.

Rook growled through his fangs at him as all of his teeth sharpened and turned crimson in response to the anger that blazed in his veins.

The angel was trespassing, should at least have the decency to harbour even the smallest flicker of fear or doubt in his eyes. The way the angel treated Hell as if he was allowed to roam it freely, without consequence, had riled Rook the moment he had met him centuries ago. It had only irritated him more each time he had seen the angel after that.

Coupled with the fact this angel seemed able to withstand the Devil's voice, even went as far as challenging his master at times, throwing curses back at him, the male really pissed him off.

Rook rolled his shoulders and didn't hold back the rage pouring through his veins. He let it flow over him and carry him away, stoked it as he narrowed his now-crimson eyes on the male. The angel dared to stand before him, to linger in his presence without fear. Worse than that, he dared to do it unarmed.

The bastard was taunting him.

Rook wasn't going to stand for it.

The male thought himself powerful, believed himself able to handle Rook without a weapon to aid him.

Rook was going to show him what a mistake all his beliefs were.

He felt it as his bones lengthened in response to the hunger to eradicate the angel that was rapidly becoming his nemesis, to free himself of the irritation of the male so he could return his focus to claiming command of the First Battalion. He growled through his all-sharp teeth again as a shadow swept over his skin, turning it black, and he continued to grow, the angel appearing to move further away as Rook transformed into his demonic form.

As the crimson rolled down Rook's feathers like blood to drip from their tips, leaving them onyx, the angel reacted at last.

A flicker of something that looked like remorse danced across his blue eyes as they shifted to Rook's wings, as he watched the feathers fall away to reveal the dark dragon-like form they concealed.

Rook spread those wings and bared his teeth at the male as he drew the weapon hanging from his waist. It transformed as he swept his hand over it, going from a short crimson blade to a mighty broadsword, one capable of cleaving the angel in two with a single stroke.

The angel's eyes leaped to it as Rook wrapped his other hand around the elongated hilt and brought it down before him, a pounding urge to relieve the angel of his head rushing through him.

That remorse lingered in their blue depths.

Rook snarled again.

Fear should be the only emotion the angel was feeling. Sheer terror that his life was about to end now that Rook stood before him in his demonic guise, a form that granted him more power than he commanded in his angelic one.

When another emotion joined the remorse in the angel's eyes, Rook launched from the spire of rock with such force it shattered, a sound like the crack of lightning echoing around Hell as he shot towards the angel, determined to end him.

Because no one pitied him.

He was strong. He beat his wings. He had worked his way through the ranks of the Devil's angels. He beat them harder. He had commanded the Second Battalion, led them in wars against Heaven and in the mortal world. He beat them harder still. He was second in command in the First Battalion, close to his goal of leading the most fearsome legion in Hell.

He drew his sword back, his gaze focused on the angel's neck.

He would prove it to this angel, right here and right now, and the last feeling the male would know was pity and remorse for questioning his strength.

He swung and he swung hard, his aim true, and grinned as his blade closed in on the angel's throat.

"Rook."

That word, uttered in a calm way that was such a contrast to the maelstrom of emotion whirling inside him, halted him in the air as surely as a sword through his heart might have. He stared down at his chest, sure he would find a blade piercing it as pain shot outwards from the centre of it, had his hands trembling and broadsword rattling just inches from the angel.

"What the *fuck?*" he snarled and beat his wings, shot backwards away from the angel to regroup and get the sudden flood of feelings that poured through him under control.

They swirled and collided, all of them birthed by hearing this angel utter his name. He understood none of them, not where they came from or what they meant, couldn't untangle the web of them no matter how hard he tried.

Rook swept his blade down by this side and growled as he realised the angel was playing him for a fool. It was all a trick. An elaborate one. The bastard wanted to lure him into a trap of some kind. How many others like Rook had this angel killed and returned to Heaven, taking their free will from them?

He served the Devil because he wanted to serve him.

This realm was his home, his entire world.

The hilt of his sword clanked against his armour as he instinctively reached for his forearm in response to that and the niggling sensation that something else had been his entire world once.

Heaven?

He shunned that thought. Even if somewhere else had been his entire world once, Hell was that place for him now. Nothing would change that.

"I know you." The angel took a step towards him, the fires of Hell reflecting off the gold edges of his black armour that moulded to his upper chest, forearms and shins, and the pointed strips that protected his hips. "I know you, Rook. It was long ago, many centuries now. I thought you dead... foolish, I see that now. Or perhaps you did die... a part of you died and it led to you serving this place."

Rook spread his wings and beat them again, not to move away from the angel but to hold a position in the air above him. He wouldn't run from this male, wouldn't allow his poisonous words to taint his heart and dissolve his strength. They were all lies, designed to weaken him.

"Any angel could discover my name," he spat and narrowed his crimson eyes on the male. "Don't think yourself clever in your approach to attempting to be my downfall."

"Downfall?" The male's lips curled slightly, a rueful edge to his smile. "Your downfall is not me, and it is not now. It happened all those centuries ago... the night you chose to serve this wretched realm."

Rook growled at that, flashing his fangs. "You know nothing of me... your realm is the wretched one, and your kind are foul fiends, determined to place my kind in Heaven's shackles again."

"I do not want to kill you, Rook." The male shook his head, a slight frown furrowing his brow. "It would defeat the purpose of my being here."

There was a glimmer of something in the male's blue eyes that said he had considered killing him at one point though. For what reason? And why hadn't he gone through with that plan?

"Why are you here then?" Rook let his demonic form fade away to conserve his strength. It was taxing to use it, wore him out even when he was in Hell, a place that was his home. His entire world. His fingers twitched with a need that he suppressed. "If not to taunt me and lure me to a place where you can murder me?"

"I needed to speak with you."

Him in particular?

"So speak, and then leave." He swept his hand back up his blade to shorten it, but kept it out, gripped at his side in case he needed it.

He tried to deny the curiosity growing inside him, but its grip on him was as fierce as his on his sword, and he found himself wanting to hear what had brought the angel into Hell and to him.

"The witch—"

"Again with this witch?" Rook cut him off.

Why did the angel keep bringing up this witch?

His free hand twitched.

He ignored it.

"She needs your help, Rook." The male took another step forwards, closer to him, and tilted his head up, causing his ponytail to slip from the shoulder of his black armour.

Armour that so closely matched Rook's own. Strange how an angel who served Heaven could be given such dark armour and wings. It hardly seemed fitting. All the angels who worked near the pool were of this male's kind though. Rook had only seen one mediator, angels with white wings, in his time. That male had come with this one a few months ago, and Rook had watched them until the Devil had grown furious and had ordered him away from them.

"You help her. I'm not interested." He went to turn away as a pressing need to leave built inside him.

The Devil exerting his will on him.

He felt it as a tug in his chest, one that had him wanting to move to a distance and call on his legion. He didn't need to call to them. They were already coming. He could feel it in his blood. Soon, this angel would be facing the strongest battalion serving Hell.

This time, Rook wouldn't let the angel flee.

"I cannot find her." The angel shifted his foot forwards, looking as if he might risk another step, and then clenched his fists at his sides and loosed a black curse. "Listen to me, Rook. She needs *you*. Only you can find her. I believe that."

Rook chuckled at that. "You believe it? I am expected to go along with your beliefs? I don't think so. I recommend you leave now."

The male stared him down, his blue eyes sober and serious. "You believed in her once."

He froze again, the collision of feelings he couldn't grasp sending his mind swirling. Had he known the witch the angel spoke of? His free hand twitched, and this time he didn't hold it back. He brushed his fingers over the raised crimson crossed axes on his vambrace and down over the skull below them.

Had he known her?

He searched his memories and found none of a witch. He had never met one of her kind before. The angel was mistaken.

Dark words rang in his mind, his order clear. Make the male leave now or face the consequences of disobedience.

Rook swept his palm down the length of his blade again, transforming it back into his crimson broadsword. He beat his scarlet feathered wings, focused his mind and readied himself.

"Will you listen to me?" the angel barked. "Do not listen to him. He wants you here for some reason. Rook, you *must* listen to me."

He growled, baring his sharp teeth, and gripped his sword in both hands. "I know no witch. I have never met one of her kind. I do not have to listen to you because you mean to deceive me."

"Fine, Rook." The male rose to his full height, tipping his chin up as his blue eyes brightened, glowing in the low light. He held his hands out in front of him and twin curved golden blades appeared in them. "We will do this the hard way."

Rook readied his own sword.

The angel unleashed his black wings, twisted away from him and beat them, hurling a wave of dust at Rook as he shot into the distance.

Rook snarled and gave chase, his wings beating furiously as he fought to close the distance between them. He was damned if he was going to let the angel get away again. This time, the male was going down. He would capture the creature and present him to the Devil, and his master would recognise his strength and skill.

The position of next commander of the First Battalion would be secured.

Everything he had ever wanted in life would be his.

His wrists burned and he grunted as a wave of fire encircled them, chasing around them beneath his vambraces and searing his bones.

It was all he wanted.

This realm was his everything.

He gritted his teeth against the ribbons of fire as they blazed hotter.

His entire world.

He squeezed his eyes shut.

A feminine voice echoed in the darkness, cutting through the pain.

It reached to him and wrapped him in comforting arms that stole it all away, left him drifting in the shadows, feeling light inside.

"I'll be with you forever."

Heat streaked down his cheeks as tremendous pain welling up inside him, agony he couldn't contain.

He threw his head back and roared.

A single thought crystallised as he emptied his lungs in a desperate attempt to purge the pain that was tearing him to pieces, threatening to consume and destroy him.

The owner of that voice was his entire world.

It shattered as quickly as it had formed.

Rook frowned down at his wrists as he beat his wings to keep him in the air. The breeze from them cooled his face for some reason. He lifted his free hand and brushed his fingers across the wetness on his cheeks, canted his head and studied it as he brought them away.

It meant nothing.

He shifted his gaze from them and fixed it on the retreating angel.

A male who would be his prize and would secure his elevation in the ranks.

He flapped his wings and shot after him, because achieving the position of commander of the First Battalion and the power it would gain him was the only thing he cared about.

It meant everything.

It was his entire world.

The only forever he desired.

BOUND ANGEL

Second in command of the most fearsome legion of fallen angels in Hell, Rook only cares about one thing—seizing control of the First Battalion and moving one step closer to the Devil. But a dark angel of Heaven keeps seeking him out, insisting a witch needs his help, and one glance at an image of the ethereal silver-haired beauty stirs powerful emotions long forgotten and rouses a deep need he cannot deny or understand—one that commands him to risk everything and save her.

Isadora has been a fool. Millennia alone, enduring an eternal life created by the bond she shares with the angel she lost, has taken its toll on her. Desperate to see a familiar face, she followed rumours to Paris and placed her trust in a group of witches, only to be betrayed once again. Now, they want the spell that has made her immortal and she's close to breaking... until a formidable warrior with crimson wings comes to her rescue, awakening old feelings never forgotten in her shattered heart.

With the mounting threat of witches and an enemy of old in danger of tearing them apart, can Rook untangle the truth about the past he can't remember and can Isadora convince her demonic angel the forever he desires is the one he promised her?

Available in ebook and paperback

ABOUT THE AUTHOR

Felicity Heaton is a New York Times and USA Today best-selling author who writes passionate paranormal romance books. In her books she creates detailed worlds, twisting plots, mind-blowing action, intense emotion and heart-stopping romances with leading men that vary from dark deadly vampires to sexy shape-shifters and wicked werewolves, to sinful angels and hot demons!

If you're a fan of paranormal romance authors Lara Adrian, J R Ward, Sherrilyn Kenyon, Kresley Cole, Gena Showalter, Larissa Ione and Christine Feehan then you will enjoy her books too.

If you love your angels a little dark and wicked, her best-selling Her Angel romance series is for you. If you like strong, powerful, and dark vampires then try the Vampires Realm romance series or any of her stand alone vampire romance books. If you're looking for vampire romances that are sinful, passionate and erotic then try her London Vampires romance series. Or if you like hot-blooded alpha heroes who will let nothing stand in the way of them claiming their destined woman then try her Eternal Mates series. It's packed with sexy heroes in a world populated by elves, vampires, fae, demons, shifters, and more. If sexy Greek gods with incredible powers battling to save our world and their home in the Underworld are more your thing, then be sure to step into the world of Guardians of Hades.

If you have enjoyed this story, please take a moment to contact the author at **author@felicityheaton.com** or to post a review of the book online

Connect with Felicity:
Website – http://www.felicityheaton.com
Blog – http://www.felicityheaton.com/blog/
Twitter – http://twitter.com/felicityheaton
Facebook – http://www.facebook.com/felicityheaton
Goodreads – http://www.goodreads.com/felicityheaton
Mailing List – http://www.felicityheaton.com/newsletter.php

FIND OUT MORE ABOUT HER BOOKS AT:
http://www.felicityheaton.com

Printed in Great Britain
by Amazon

22075349R00088